Zara Cox writes

She lives in the C

with her hubby an

travel. In 2017 sh

cket list destina

eading with her husband to live there! She loves
hear from her readers and you can get in touch
ith her via Twitter (@zcoxbooks), on Instagram
zaracoxwriter) or Facebook (zaracoxwriter).

If you liked *Close to the Edge*, why not try

Beddable Billionaire by Alexx Andria
Getting Lucky by Avril Tremayne
Forbidden Pleasure by Taryn Leigh Taylor

Discover more at millsandboon.co.uk

CLOSE TO THE EDGE

ZARA COX

MILLS & BOON

First Published in Great Britain 2018
by Mills & Boon, an imprint of HarperCollins*Publishers*
1 London Bridge Street, London, SE1 9GF

© 2018 Zara Cox

ISBN: 978-0-263-93228-7

MIX
Paper from
responsible sources
FSC **C007454**

This book is produced from independently certified FSC™ paper
to ensure responsible forest management.
For more information visit www.harpercollins.co.uk/green.

Printed and bound in Spain
by CPI, Barcelona

To Grace Thiele,
for being the physical manifestation of Lily Gracen.

CHAPTER ONE

Caleb

THE QUICK GLANCE at my wrist was a bad idea. I knew the moment my gaze dropped to the black-and-azure face of my watch that I'd added another half hour to this circus.

Shit.

"Oh, am I wasting your time? Do you have somewhere *important* to be?" the whiny voice demanded.

I sighed.

The ability to turn circumstances, good or bad, to my advantage was what had earned me my renowned status. But no one starts life thinking they were going to do what I do, be what I am.

A fixer.

I wasn't complaining, though. I was great at my job. Sometimes I wish I wasn't *this* damned good… Oh, who the hell was I kidding? Most days I loved my job. Tonight, not so much. The 2 a.m. calls were the worst. Especially when they interrupted a very promising pre-fuck blowjob.

But hey, what was a small case of blue balls when the siren song of work beckoned? As evading tactics went, it was an effective way to hold the demons at bay.

I shoved my hands into my pockets and glared at the glassy-eyed man-child straddling the banister in front of me. "Yes, actually. I do have somewhere else to be. So if you're going to jump, get it over with so I can get on with my night."

Christ, you've surpassed yourself this time, Steele.

My client's slack-faced shock confirmed my thought. "Are you fucking serious?"

"As Zachary Quinto's eyebrows. This is the fourth time I've had to deal with your...unhappiness this month alone. Normally, I would've washed my hands of you or dragged you to rehab. But I promised your father I'd look out for you. The only thing you're addicted to is laziness—"

"You don't know what you're talking about. The band kicked me out!"

"Because you set your GPS to Cabo instead of your studio in Culver City. Last month it was Vegas. The month before it was Atlantic City, right?"

"I can't just turn up and sing! I need inspiration," Ross Jonas sulked.

"And you think you're going to find that by jumping off this balcony tonight?" I shrugged. "Go ahead, then. I can have you in a nice corner slab in the morgue by sunrise."

His jaw dropped again. "Holy fuck, you're something else."

I closed my eyes and wished those words were coming from a different mouth, preferably the scarlet-painted female one I'd left in my bed. When I opened them again, Ross was still there. Shame.

I wasn't twisted enough to wish my client dead but I wanted this over and done with.

He wasn't going to jump.

We'd been through this dance enough times. He chose this suite because there was a deep pool conveniently situated six floors below. And if by some exceptionally bad luck he didn't make it, I had four guys on the ground floor of the Beverly Hills Hotel ready with a giant inflatable to catch his sorry ass because sadly, this wasn't my first rodeo with a pseudo-suicidal client.

I would've dropped him as a client a long time ago, for his selfish antics for starters, and because I never took on suicidal clients, not even ones who were faking it. I wasn't ashamed to admit suicide was a red-hot button for me. But Ross's father was my first client, the guy who'd given me a break in a cutthroat place like LA, then gone out of his way to recommend my services to others. And when Victor Jonas had all but begged me to look out for his son, I'd agreed unconditionally.

The worst Ross, only child of rich, overindulgent parents, would suffer tonight if he did jump, was having the wind knocked out of him.

Whereas I was destined to suffer a stronger resurgence of the nightmares I fought each night, not to mention the cold shoulder of a pouty redhead if I didn't wrap this up fast. "Yes, I *am* something else. And *you* have ten seconds to shit or get off the pot."

I straightened from my leaning position against the French doors and moved toward him. He glanced furtively behind him and paled. "Fuck," he muttered.

Two feet away I stopped and crossed my arms. "Listen to me. You keep flirting with death like this and one day you'll succeed. Do me a favor, Ross. Put a little bit of the effort you use to jerk me around into doing some *actual* work. You might be surprised at how good it feels to reap the results of your hard work."

The belligerence drained from his face. "But I'm out of the band."

"Call your guys in the morning. Beg if you need to. Humility goes a long way if you truly mean it," I said. I had no clue whether that was true or not. Humility wasn't exactly a strong suit of mine. "And while you're at it, try showing up when you say you will. Deal?"

When he nodded I stepped back, staying alert as he slowly climbed down. Relieved, I followed him back into the suite he'd checked into for the purpose of pulling this shitty, dangerous stunt.

I breathed through the fury and resisted the urge to tear another strip off him. "One of my guys is going to stick around, make sure you get to Culver City nice and early in the morning. Sound good?"

I slapped him on the shoulder and headed for the door. With any luck, my date would still be warming my bed.

"Hey, Caleb."

I turned around. "Yeah?"

"Would you…really have watched me jump?"

My face tightened. "If you wanted to, I couldn't have stopped you." I paused a beat. "Did you?"

He shook his head sheepishly. "No."

My anger spiked another notch. "Pull a stunt like this again and I'll push you myself."

I left him standing in the middle of the living room, shoulders hunched, pondering that.

My jaw tightened as the elevator rushed me to the ground floor. Unfortunately, the memories Ross had triggered weren't as easy to leave behind as I exited the five-star hotel.

For my mother it'd been third time lucky. Or *unlucky*, depending on which side of the fence you stood on. My steps faltered as the acid-sharp pain that always accompanied the memory of her death plowed through me.

Damn Ross Jonas.

With a deep breath I walked out, handed a twenty to the valet attendant holding out the keys to my Bugatti and slid behind the wheel.

Before I could pull away, my phone beeped. Tugging it out of my pocket, I found a centerfold-worthy picture gracing my screen. The accompanying message flashed seconds later.

This is what you could've had tonight. Call me never!

I was torn between a smile and a scowl. A smile because if I chose to call her right then, she would've answered. A scowl because the redhead was the first to tweak my interest in a while, and I'd hoped she would end this uninvited dry spell that had taken over my sex life. But despite my earlier anticipation, the desire to get her back in my bed was dwindling fast. I stared at the picture again and stroked my dying wood a second before I hit the Delete button, erasing her from my contacts altogether.

I gunned the engine onto the Pacific Coast Highway, pointing my car toward Downtown LA. With my bedroom plans now shot to shit, and in no mood to return to an empty bed and dreams filled with memories I didn't cherish, work was the next best option.

Nevertheless, I cursed when my phone rang. "Dammit, doesn't anyone sleep anymore?" I griped.

Maggie, my assistant, answered, "You don't pay me to sleep. You specifically stated during my interview that I wasn't allowed to sleep."

"*You* don't get to sleep. That doesn't mean you can interrupt mine. I'm shocked I need to explain that to you."

"Tell me you're not heading to Fixer HQ right now and I'll hang up."

I didn't bother because she had a GPS tracker on my car. Once or twice that tracker had saved my skin and extricated me from some unsavory situations.

"What do you want, Maggie?" I switched lanes, enjoying the sweet purr of the engine.

"Wow, someone's grumpy," she muttered under her breath, then said briskly, "We have an urgent situation."

I tapped my finger against the wheel. "Aren't they all?"

"This one is less sex, drugs and rock and roll, more… something else."

I suppressed a growl. "By all means, hold the dramatics."

My sarcasm bounced right off her thick skin. It was one of the many reasons she was invaluable. "I'm sending you the address her people sent me. You can be there in fifteen minutes."

The joy in my ride gone, I cursed. "Her *people*? Did you not explain to them that I don't deal with *people*? That it's one-on-one or not at all?"

Maggie sighed. "I know how to do my job, Caleb. Trust me, please, just a little?"

I frowned. I didn't trust blindly because I didn't trust anyone. Maggie knew this. Why she was choosing to tap into a resource not readily available to me wasn't improving my mood. The sizeable monthly paycheck I signed bought me her hard work and loyalty. I didn't expect anything else, and certainly not her request for me to trust her.

My phone buzzed with the incoming address. "I'll be in touch." I hung up, pulled off the road long enough to check out the Mulholland Drive address before I executed a slick U-turn.

High walls and electronic gates greeted me when I reached the property. Everything about this smelled like trust-fund princess with her panties in a twist about her latest flame. Or a chihuahua kidnapping that wasn't worth my time.

Only the assurance that Maggie excelled at her job made me roll down my window and press the intercom.

The cast-iron gate slid back, and I drove up the cobbled driveway of a large stone mansion. In typical Hollywood style, the original property had been remodeled into a grotesque status symbol, with little care for artistic design.

I hid my lip curl as I stepped out and spotted the rent-a-cops stationed on either side of the house.

The front door swung open to reveal a young, sharply dressed man on the threshold. He seemed out of place in this setting but I wasn't here to judge. "Good evening, Mr. Steele. If you'll come with me?" He didn't offer his name and I didn't ask for it. This was LA, where even D-list celebrities were paranoid about revealing their identities to the wrong person.

The inside of the mansion was as gaudy as the outside, the designer having gone to town with an explosion of golds and leafy greens splashed across every surface.

Suppressing a shudder, I went down a hallway into a large living room, growing impatient when a look around didn't produce the *her* Maggie had mentioned.

"Wait here, please."

He left. I paced, silently hoping this trip would be worth my while. I had a dossier full of needy clients but their demands were nothing I couldn't handle in my sleep. Thoughts of sleep, or the woeful lack of it lately, ramped up the disquiet inside me.

I was busy smashing it down when the double doors opened in front of me.

At the first sight of her, my gut clenched tight and my lungs flattened with expelled air I wasn't interested in replenishing.

I wasn't sure whether it was the shock of her roughly chopped white-blond hair that gripped my attention or the wide, full red lips currently getting sucked between her teeth. Maybe it was the bright, oval-shaped green eyes staring directly at me. Or the lush petiteness of the body draped from head to toe in black leather and lace.

Leather and lace.

The combination was lethal enough without the silver-studded leather cuffs encircling both wrists and her slim throat.

Jesus.

She was a cross between a wannabe punk rock star and a BDSM enthusiast's wet dream.

She stared at me, our height disparity forcing her to angle her head and expose her delicate neck to me. Edgy hunger burned through me as I tracked her alabaster-pale face, the lightest flutter of her nostrils, the velvet smoothness of her mouth. The racing pulse beneath her choker.

She inhaled and exhaled slowly. "I hear you're a fixer."

"You heard correctly." I wasn't in the phone book. Referrals were strictly by word of mouth. I sent silent thanks to whichever client had sent her my way.

She gave a brisk nod. "Before we start, we need to discuss an NDA," she said in a sexy voice I wanted in surround sound in my head.

I was used to nondisclosure agreements. No one worth a damn did business these days without first whipping out an NDA. But whether it was the time of night or my general mood lately, I shook my head.

"Before we discuss NDAs I need the broad strokes of the job first." Who was I kidding? This woman, who-ever she was, intrigued me. I was fairly sure I was going to take the job.

Her mouth firmed. "Fair enough. I've picked up a stalker," she said matter-of-factly. "It started off as cyberstalking but in the past three weeks it's escalated to physical stalking."

The bolt of unexpected protectiveness shot through me, unsettling me enough to make me cross my arms. "And you haven't called the cops because…?"

"Because it could be linked with the work I'm doing."

"What work?"

"Extremely sensitive work that I can't discuss with-out you signing the NDA." She held out the document.

My intrigue spiked. "Okay, let's see it."

It was seven pages long, far more detailed than the standard three-page NDA, with her name left blank. I noticed her studying me from the corner of my eye as I read it a second time. When I was done, I shifted my gaze to her, my interest mounting when she met my eye boldly. "It looks good. Pen?"

As if on cue, the door opened, and the young guy who opened the front door walked in. I watched him, then her, looking for signs of a relationship. She nodded her thanks when he produced a pen, but there was nothing else in her gaze that tweaked my senses.

I grimaced at the relief that shot through me, and signed.

She took the pen and inserted her name.

Lily Angela Gracen.

I stared at the name, searched the corners of my mind and came up empty as the guy witnessed the document.

As she walked him to the door I allowed myself a second, more intimate look.

Hell, she was *stunning.*

No one deserved to be stalked, online or in real life, but *fuck*, looking at her, I understood why she could become an object of some psycho's obsession.

The moment the thought crossed my mind, I froze, rejecting the idea of her being in danger, even while my cock stirred to life, excited by the magnificent vision crossing the room toward me.

She moved with understated but sexy awareness, a woman who acknowledged her considerable attributes but didn't need to flaunt them. A woman who knew the power of those curvy hips, her plump lips and generous breasts.

Despite her combat boots adding a couple of inches to her height, she barely came up to my chest. Petite, perfectly proportioned, she was the epitome of a filthy, decadent Pocket Venus.

She probably weighed no more than a hundred and

ten pounds. On a good day I bench-pressed twice her weight. My mind reeled with images of how she would feel in my arms.

Easily pinned against a wall, her naked, delicious weight trapped between my greedy hands.

Easily tied down to a bed with silk ropes if that was her thing, her skin flushed pink as she straddled the fine line between preorgasmic tension and a screaming climax.

Easily subdued and tossed into the back of a van by some unhinged asshole with entitlement issues.

I yanked myself away from lurid sexual scenarios and adjusted my stance to ease the constriction in my pants as the most gorgeous creature I'd seen in a long time stopped before me.

"Who was he?" I nodded at the door.

"He came with the house rental. I asked him to stick around to witness the document."

"Okay, now that I've signed your document, let's start again. I'm Caleb Steele. Fixer."

She stared at the hand I held out. "Lily Gracen, chief coder for Sierra Donovan Media."

Despite what was happening to her, she had more than a little sass. And if she was a coder, she had brains, too. A lethal combination on any given day. Packaged in that body, I got the strongest suspicion I was in for an exhilarating ride.

After several moments she took my hand.

The second I felt the warm sizzle of her flesh, experienced an extra shot of testosterone through my system and watched her eyes widen in mutual acknowledgment of the rush, I accepted my reality. Signed NDA or not, the unholy fire spreading through my bloodstream had only one destination.

I was going to cross a helluva lot of lines, all of which started and ended with one fact.

I was going to fuck Lily Angela Gracen.

CHAPTER TWO

Caleb

WHOA. TAKE IT down a notch or six, cowboy.

Getting involved with Lily Gracen while she was my client had *bad idea* written all over it. I'd learned that lesson the hard way.

Which was why I broke my rules for no one.

A fixer's first and last defense against failure was his neutrality. Starting out I'd disregarded that by getting involved with Kirsten. A young actress on the precarious rise, her cultivated vulnerability had slipped beneath my guard, triggered emotions she'd expertly manipulated to suit her purposes. Emotions that had turned me into a laughingstock and nearly tanked my reputation.

Never again were two words I abided by.

Already, my sexual attraction to Lily Gracen was getting in the way of that neutrality. And that bite of protectiveness the moment I saw her? That needed to go, as well. My task was to find her stalker without messy emotions getting in the way.

But...once that was done, there would be nothing stopping me from rewarding myself with a taste of her.

Yeah, I wasn't perfect. At no point in my life did I try to be. You can't go countless rounds in the boxing ring of life without emerging with a few scars both inside and out.

I'd dragged myself from the rougher parts of South Central LA and into the twenty-thousand square feet of a Malibu mansion via some seriously rocky terrain, experiencing every imaginable facet of human nature along the way.

It was the reason I now lived by three simple rules:

Protect the innocent and vulnerable at all cost. Always.

No sleeping with clients, no matter how tempting.

No sleeping with the fucking clients, no matter how fucking *tempting.*

The foundation of rule one would never waver. I feared for the foundation of rules two and three as I held on to Lily's hand, drifted my thumb across one satin-smooth knuckle. She gratified my touch with a sharp catch of her breath.

God, I wanted to hear that sound louder, preferably preceding a scream as I buried my cock inside her sweet little pussy.

But first, I needed to get down to business.

She beat me to it by tugging her hand out of mine. "Shall we discuss the details?"

As she walked away, I caught the scent of her perfume—earthy, evocative of rain-soaked heather, the kind that invited you to roll around in when the sun came out. I wanted to follow that scent with my nose. And then with my hands and my mouth.

Down boy, I cautioned my cock when it jumped in agreement.

"Sure."

She sat down at one end of the sofa, crossed her legs and waved me to the seat next to her. "Sit down, Mr. Steele."

The take-charge attitude from such a diminutive person was an unexpected turn-on. I let her have the leeway. For now.

I sat, dragging my gaze from her shapely calves and thighs. "One thing you should know—I won't be managed. If you want me to catch this…person, you'll let me do my job."

She stared at me for a moment, then shrugged. "We'll get to that in a moment."

Again, I tried not to react like a horny teenager to the sound of her voice, but God, it was something else. Hell, from the top of those roughly chopped locks to the tips of her boots, she was something else.

"Is Steele really your last name?" she asked abruptly, her slender arms folded.

I raised an eyebrow. "Do you always go out dressed like that?" Okay, not how I'd wanted to start, but it was a pertinent question. I didn't have a problem with the way any woman dressed, but some guys out there were sick enough to form vile opinions about women based on the way they dressed.

Her pointy little chin rose. "What's wrong with the way I dress?"

I laughed, absently noting how the sound scraped my throat. "Nothing to me. But everything to the wrong person."

She inhaled sharply. "What does that mean?"

"That I hope your stalker is the type who's just obsessed with your outer appearance. Those are the easiest to catch because they can't help themselves. They'll slip up and attempt to make physical contact with you sooner rather than later."

A tiny shiver went through her but her gaze didn't waver. "Why are you assuming the stalker's interest is sexual?"

"Because I have eyes. You're a fucking knockout. But if you say it's not, I'm willing to delay a final verdict on the bastard until I hear all the facts."

A light blush bloomed into her cheeks. From the way her lips pressed together I could tell she hated that little evidence of her emotions. I enjoyed it a little too much. "Are you always this blunt?" she asked.

I folded my arms to prevent them from doing something stupid. Like tracing that blush down to her throat. "Always. That going to be problem?"

Her small fingers gripped her biceps. "Only if you don't like having it reciprocated."

"I'm good with blunt. I prefer it, even. And yes, Steele is really my name."

It was one of the few facts my mother blessed me with in the midst of her dark despair; and one of the first things I did when I established solid, reliable contacts through my work was to find the man whose blood coursed through my veins. Turned out I came from a long line of mostly no-good Steeles. A shocking percentage had been criminals. Of those that were alive, including my father, I wanted nothing to do with in this lifetime.

I refocused on her as she recrossed her legs, and I couldn't stop myself from staring. The hem of her black leather skirt had ridden up to midthigh, and she was making no move to pull it down. That tiny bit of exhibitionism ramped up my temperature another hundred notches. My tongue grew thicker and I watched her foot bounce for several seconds before I realized she was waiting for me to speak.

I cleared my throat and forced my brain back on the right track. "You think your stalker isn't interested in you personally. So it's work related?"

"I think so."

"Okay. Tell me about the project you're working on."

She hesitated.

"I need to know where to start looking. Who to rule out," I pushed.

She toyed with the tiny spikes on her wrist cuff as she weighed her words. "It's an algorithm that significantly comprises data. On a small scale it can store almost fifteen times as much data as on the ordinary thirty-two-gigabyte chip you use on your phone."

Okay, that blew my mind a little. But I suspected my mind was about to be blown even further. "And on a larger scale?"

"If our planned launch is successful next month, it can render almost all the current data storage algorithms obsolete in under a year." She spoke with quiet but fierce pride.

I gave a low whistle. "And you wrote the code? All of it?"

There was no false modesty. Just a firm nod. "Yes. It's all mine."

"That's impressive."

Her gaze rose from her wrist to mine. The determined fire and pride that burned in her eyes said she knew what she was capable of, and was hell-bent on going after it. I could see how that would piss a few male egos off.

"Thank you," she responded in a low, husky voice.

Impossibly, the evidence of power she held in her small body and that huge brain of hers turned me on even more. I was a greedy enough asshole to admit that I wanted to experience what that power blazing through her felt like. I wanted to see her drunk on it, if only for a moment, so I could feel the intoxicating afterburn of it.

But that urge would have to be curtailed for a while because, unfortunately, her revelation had thrown open several avenues where the threat could be coming from.

I rose, thankful that with the much bigger problem on my mind, my body was calming down a little from its sexual frenzy. Although I still needed to turn away to hide the semi-erection throbbing behind my fly. I was crossing the room when I heard her question.

"Is something wrong?"

I glanced at her over my shoulder. "That depends on how wide your circle of trust is. And how wide *their* circles are. I suggest we get things moving sooner rather than later." I pulled out my phone and was about to hit the first number on my speed dial when it blared to life.

Maggie's uncanny timing was impressive. But not if she was calling with anything that might distract me from Lily Gracen.

"Yes?" My voice was terser than I intended, but what the hell. The night was turning out to be interesting in some ways and extremely frustrating in others.

"Just checking in. On the off chance I blew it, I wanted to know if I should tender my resignation now or get some sleep and do it in the morning," Maggie said with a pinch of sarcasm that straddled the fine line between amusing and insubordinate.

But despite my irritation, I toyed with giving her a bonus for landing me this job.

"We have a new client."

"Yes! Great job, Maggie. I've no idea what I'd do without you, Maggie. I'll even consider giving you that pay raise you've been hinting at for the last six months, Maggie."

"Keep talking about yourself in the third person and your boss will think you're a lunatic and fire your ass."

"I don't want that. At all. What do you need me to do?" she asked, back in my preferred super-efficient mode.

I strolled to the farthest window while I updated Maggie on the assignment. "My first thought was to keep her completely off the radar while I hunted down this creep, but I've changed my mind."

"O…kay."

"I need you to prepare a couple of safe houses. Have the jet on standby, too. We might need to change location quickly."

"Yes, boss. Right away, boss."

"Don't be a smart-ass, Maggie."

"Absolutely not. Safe houses. Private jet. Check."

"Good girl. And if you insist on it, you can go get some sleep after that. But I need you bright and early in the morning. Got it?"

"Of course. I'll text you once it's done."

I hung up, satisfied with taking the direct approach to Lily's problem.

I turned around. She'd stopped messing with her cuff, but her fingers were linked over one knee, and the look in her eyes was mildly censorious.

"You have something to say?"

"Do you treat all your employees like that?"

I pocketed my phone. "Like what?"

"Like they're one level up from chattels."

I retraced my steps back to her. "I don't have a problem cracking the whip, if that's what you mean. I find it works best if it's established clearly who's boss." I didn't add that Maggie often rolled her eyes when I used my dominant voice. Which was pretty much all the time.

"So that's your thing? You like to lord it over people?"

I shoved my hands in my pockets as I stood over her. This time the disparity was even more acute, and her upturned face was even more exposed. Fuck, she was so small, such a delicious morsel wrapped in a bundle of sharp brains and fierce beauty. That feral urge to possess her stormed through me, firing up every cell in my body.

Still, I should probably have curbed the words that slid to the tip of my tongue. But hell, I was never one to back down from speaking my mind. I'd learned the hard way how high the cost of holding my tongue could be.

"Would you like me to lord it over you, sweetheart?"

Her eyes widened into alluring green pools. Her nostrils pinched delicately as she inhaled too quickly. "Excuse me?"

"I will, Lily Gracen, but only if you ask me very, very nicely."

Lily

There were so many things wrong with his statement that I didn't know where to start. I wasn't even sure where shock ended and annoyance started. Which was surprising since for the past three years I'd lived in an environment dominated by the worst type of male ego—one with a half-decent brain and a bottomless bank account.

Silicon Valley wasn't the place for shrinking violets, and while my start at SDM may not have been conventional, I soon learned to find my voice or be flattened by pompous assholes.

That voice was now trapped somewhere between my throat and my tongue as I stared up at the seriously gorgeous man planted before me, watching me with eyes that started saucy little fires in my body.

I cleared my throat. "You're forgetting who hired whom, Mr. Steele. Technically, I'm your boss. If anyone will be *lording* anything, it'll be me."

For some reason that made his piercing blue eyes gleam. "I don't have a problem with a woman calling the shots. Within reason, of course."

Between his eyes and his deep, sexy, gravel-rough voice, I forgot, for a moment, the sinister threats hanging over my head, jeopardizing everything I'd worked hard for. I was so close to living my life on my terms. To being free of the devil's bargain my stepfather had struck with my employer to keep me shackled.

But staring at Caleb Steele, the deep unease I'd been bottling down since my stalker's first contact faded a little, enough for me to experience new, equally unsettling sensations.

The thinly disguised sexual interest in his eyes had lit a fire beneath my skin from the moment our eyes met. I knew the way I chose to dress, the individual statement I made with my hair and clothes, meant I attracted looks that my younger, teenage self would've shied away from. But that was before I was forced to grow a hard shell. Before it became clear that no matter what I did, all I would ever be was a monthly check to my stepfather for the meager attention grudgingly tossed my way through years of bitter, enforced parenting, and a means of harnessing my talent from Chance Donovan, the man I worked for.

But freedom was within my grasp.

Once I got rid of my stalker problem.

Somewhere in a place I refused to visit very often, the sting of rejection resided. But that pain had diminished significantly over time. In fact, I discovered the neat little trick that the more I worked the less I thought about my dismal past.

Except that work was now in jeopardy. The jagged circle of thought brought me back to my solution—Caleb Steele.

The man who stood before me was a tower of raw masculinity and unapologetic dominance.

His dark blue eyes were commanding to the point of hypnotic, and he dripped the kind of sexual assurance that very few men could carry off.

As for the impressive bulge I glimpsed as he strolled across the room a few minutes ago…?

I pressed my suddenly hot thighs together, struggled not to drop my gaze to the part of his anatomy that was unnervingly close to my face and cursed the blush creeping my neck.

You have a stalker, *Lily Angela Gracen. The last thing you should be thinking about is how incredible it would be to give your first blowjob to this drop-dead gorgeous man who's staring at you as if he wants to take a very big, very greedy, bite out of you.*

I stepped back from the edge of insanity as he leaned down, bringing his impressive height and stunning physique closer.

"Lily… Can I call you Lily?" he asked in that insanely sexy voice.

Enough already. My control may be slipping from me in other areas of my life. I wasn't going to let it slip here. "No. You can't. You haven't earned that right."

He raised one sleek, dark eyebrow, and hell, even that small action was crazy-hot. And when he smiled, his eyes gleamed with a new, carnal light that threatened to set me on fire all over again. "I don't usually go in for the brownie points system but if that's what turns you on…" He shrugged.

I frowned. "You misunderstand. Deliberately, I suspect. We're not discussing what turns me on. Or…having you lord…whatever over me." *Thanks, brain, for choosing today to deliver my speech in stupid ellipses!* "That's not going to happen, either, by the way, just so we're clear. *I'm* all about having this problem handled, ASAP, so I can get on with my life. Plus, I'm friendly with people I trust, and I don't trust you." There. Direct and to the point.

"You don't trust me…yet. That's okay. I'm skeptical, too. For instance, I'm not totally convinced that a bodyguard or a private investigator can't handle this job. So, Lily…how are *you* going to convince *me* to get off the fence?"

I hated the ground-shifting sensation that came with the idea that he could walk away. My research had indicated he was the man for the job. I didn't have time to find another. "You want me to pay you double? Is that it?"

The snap of irritation in his eyes indicated I'd caused offense. My stomach knotted harder.

"I turn away three out of five clients. Money isn't an issue for me. If you want me, do better."

"Fine. I was told you're the best of the best. I need the best."

He didn't answer for several drawn-out seconds. His hands returned to his pockets, and he rocked on his feet before he nodded. "Great. You've got me."

Convinced the loaded words were just in my mind, I ignored the heat pooling in my pelvis and pressed on. "It's almost two in the morning. Every second that passes is a second I'm being kept from doing my job. So can we proceed, Mr. Steele?"

"Does anyone else know you're being stalked?"

"Not yet, but if the threats continue I'll have to inform Chance Donovan. He's my boss and CEO of SDM."

Thoughts of Chance cooled my churning jets. As the moneyman behind my project, he was under pressure from his board of directors to deliver the code on time. Over the past month, that pressure had been redirected my way, with hints of the unpleasant consequences should I fail to meet my deadline.

"I'm hoping you'll fix my problem before that becomes necessary."

Caleb nodded, and I caught a different gleam in his

eyes. Respect. Maybe a little admiration. For some absurd reason, pleasure fizzed through me.

"I was going to suggest a safe house but I'm guessing you'll draw attention to your absence if you don't show up at work?"

"Yes. Usually, I can come and go as I please, but I have a team working with me."

His eyes narrowed. "A team?"

"The algorithm I'm building is huge. I have three teams of three working independently on different aspects of the code to minimize leaking of confidential information. They all report to me."

"So they don't know exactly what you're working on?" he fired at me.

"No." That had been Chance's idea. One I disagreed with but had no choice but to accept.

My expression must have given me away because Caleb frowned. "What aren't you telling me?"

My gut told me Caleb was the kind of guy who needed full disclosure or he might walk. "Chance and I have a history."

"What kind?"

"I was fourteen when I…came to his attention."

His gaze stayed fixed on me. "Let me guess. You hacked him. He caught you and convinced you to work for him instead."

A cute anecdote except for the part where I became tied to my so-called savior via a thousand wires made of veiled threats. I tightened the knots of pain and bitterness threatening to unravel. "Something like that," I replied. "Anyway, I can't be away from Sunnyvale for long. Which is why I'm going back tonight. What I want to know is will you be coming with me?"

A hard glint entered his eyes. "I will. On one condition. If we're going into your stalker's territory, you'll agree to do things my way, including letting me step into a situation if I think it's for your own good."

"But—"

"No buts. It says so in the small print of my retainer."

We faced off, a vortex of thunder and lightning swirling around us, eddying us dangerously closer. "It said I had to relinquish reasonable power to you. Not *all* power."

"*'There will be times when the fixer may have to take an* act-first-explain-later *approach to a situation. The client agrees to comply if such a situation arises.'* Did you make a note of that line?" His voice was low but deadly soft.

"Sure, I read that part. And you're probably used to having your every mandate agreed to immediately. Unfortunately, you and I will have a big problem if you insist on being...rigid."

"I can be as flexible as any situation demands. But not in this case. You forget. You *need* me."

I hated my words being thrown back in my face. Almost as much as I'd hated the thought of hiring a bodyguard and waiting the stalker out.

I was weeks from being free of Chance and my stepfather. The thought of adding even an extra hour's delay to that liberating moment was unacceptable. Still, relinquishing control was hard. "Do you find a client taking charge of their own safety a deal breaker for you?"

My question seemed to throw him off. A tiny frown pleated his brow, and then his striking blue gaze left mine to scour my body before returning to my face. As I watched, he reeled himself in. Like the man, his expression was fascinating to watch. It was as if he'd been in danger of overstepping a line and had coldly and ruthlessly corrected his course.

"No, but if you want an obedient thug, feel free to pick one of those rent-a-cops outside."

"All right. If you're up to something more challenging, then I agree to your terms."

The direct taunt to his supposedly flawless record—and yes, to his ego—was one I made with my breath held tight. For reasons I couldn't fathom, I hated the thought of him walking away even more.

With a single step, he closed the gap between us and lowered his lips to my ear. "Be very careful where you throw your little gauntlets, Lily Gracen. One might come back to bite you in your delectable ass."

It was impossible to stop the hot little shiver that raced through me. He saw it, and a bright blue flame lit his eyes.

"Well, be warned. I bite back."

"This is going to be very interesting," he mused. Then without taking his eyes from mine, he reached for his phone. I heard faint ringing in the background before it was answered.

"Maggie, is the primary crew in place?"

"Yes, they'll land in Palo Alto in thirty minutes. They can be at Miss Gracen's house in an hour. Do we have a green light?"

He lowered the phone. "Do I have the green light, Lily?"

"Your team is already in San Francisco. So you intended to take my case all along?"

He shrugged. "I needed to make sure you were fully committed but I saw no reason not to start the ball rolling."

I took a steadying breath. "I don't appreciate being toyed with, Mr. Steele."

All traces of humor left his face. "Then we're in total agreement because this is no fucking joke."

His harsh reply tightened the skin on my nape, warned me there was something else going on here.

"My guys are waiting," he pressed. "All they'll be doing tonight is setting up a few cameras outside the property and scoping out the area. They're experts, trustworthy, handpicked by me. They won't rifle through your underwear drawer or whatever naughty things you keep in your closet if that's what you're worried about. So, do I have the green light, Lily?" That last bit was muttered with a hot little taunt as his gaze raked my face.

I fought to hold on to my irritation and dismiss the tiny lick of embarrassment.

So okay, I wasn't the tidiest person at the best of times. And being neck-deep in my project, I'd let my standards slip a little further and canceled my cleaning service because I hated the disruption. Which meant any number of personal items, including the ones I used to de-stress after a hard day's coding, could be scattered anywhere in my house.

The joy of living alone meant I could pleasure myself anywhere from my bathroom floor to the movie room lounger where I usually crashed when I couldn't be bothered to drag myself to my bed. The thought of Caleb Steele's men reporting my habits back to him made my palms burn with humiliation.

Which was absurd.

I was a grown woman, for heaven's sake. One with healthy needs I wasn't ashamed of satisfying in defiance of the restrictions Chance Donovan had tried to place on me.

Nope, I wasn't going to think about Chance or how he tried to control me through Scott, my ex-boyfriend.

Very soon they'd both be so far in my rearview I'd need a telescope to see them.

"You have the green light," I said, blanking my mind to the possibility of my sex toys being discovered. "You'll need a code to get into the house."

The small cocky smile that curved his lips suggested that he really didn't, but he chose not to vocalize the fact. "Shoot."

I rattled out a long alphanumeric code. He impressed me by not asking me to repeat it and recited it to Maggie without hesitation.

About to hang up, he paused when Maggie called his name. "Yes?"

"The pilot is still on standby. I'm assuming you and the client are returning to Palo Alto, too?"

"Yes, we'll be at the airport in half an hour." He hung up, the blue of his eyes drenching me with the sensation of being swallowed whole. "Come on. Let's go get this bastard out of your life."

I grabbed my things and followed Caleb Steele outside with the distinct feeling he'd left out a vital part of his statement. Something along the lines of...*and then we can get onto more important things*.

Or maybe that was all in *my* dirty imagination.

CHAPTER THREE

Lily

IT WASN'T THE first time I'd ridden in a Bugatti—Silicon Valley was crawling with billionaire tech geeks who collected supercars like they were baseball cards.

But it was the first time I'd ridden in a supercar driven by a man like Caleb Steele. And this, too, was turning out to be a sex-steeped experience.

The man drove his car like he was making love to it. Scratch that. He drove like he was fucking it. Smooth. Sexy. Relentless. Each flick of the gear and flex of his thigh as he switched from gas to brake was a hypnotic symphony. One so absorbing I couldn't look away.

I realized my lip was caught between my teeth, and my fingers were digging into the soft leather, and forced myself to release both. To take a breath unfortunately filled with sandalwood and prime male, in order to get my brain on track.

Caleb Steele was the type of guy who would see my discomfort as a weakness and use it to his advantage.

"Where are we flying from?" He'd been mostly silent since we left the mansion. Admittedly, I found it a little disconcerting, especially since I'd anticipated being peppered with questions.

He changed lanes again before he answered, sending me a sidelong glance that left me with that faint impression of what being electrocuted by a low current would feel like. Even after he looked away, I experienced aftershocks.

"Van Nuys Airport. Don't worry, petal. I'll have you home in no time."

"I don't like pet names, Mr. Steele."

"You don't like pet names and you don't want me to use your first name. The only way I'm calling you *Miss Gracen* is if we're role-playing naughty teacher/stern principal."

I was gripping the seat again. *Dammit.* I forced myself to uncurl my fingers before I damaged them because I needed them to write code. "Maybe this wasn't such a great idea, after all."

Watchful blue eyes gleamed wickedly in the lights from the dashboard. "Sorry, baby, it's too late to change your mind. You're stuck with me."

Baby. Sweetheart. Petal. He probably had an endless list of pet names he tossed at women.

Short of lowering myself to his level and calling him Big Guy or Sexy Ass or Hot Rod, I had to concede this round. "Fine, you can call me Lily. Because, heaven forbid, you run out of pet names and start calling me *honey cheeks*."

"Thank you, Lily," he said in a low, deep voice that rumbled over me like delicious hot fudge over a sundae. "And by the way, I would never peg you as honey cheeks. Not with that flawless pale skin." That slow-building, insanely sexy smile returned. "Is it deliberate?"

"Is what deliberate?"

"Your paleness. It works well with the Goth vibe but it must be hell to avoid the sun when you live in California."

"What does the paleness of my skin have to do with the case?" *Or anything else that doesn't make me think of sex?*

"Zilch. This is insatiable curiosity on my part. So?"

"So, you'll just have to accept that it won't be satisfied this time."

"Shame," he murmured. "I'll just have to use my imagination."

I averted my gaze, but I was still thinking about that smile, the effortless sensuality he wove into the most innocuous words, when he swung the powerful sports car onto the exit ramp leading to the airport.

After passing through security, Caleb drove into a brightly lit hangar and parked next to a gleaming white jet. Its steps were lowered, the engine humming. The pilot and copilot were talking to two airport officials as we alighted but my attention was drawn to the woman standing at the bottom of the steps.

Her short, sequined silver tube dress, long silver necklaces and rows of hooped earrings ruled her out as an attendant. She was shrugging into a bomber jacket when Caleb stepped out and came around to open my door.

"Do we need to discuss appropriate work attire again?" His tone was bone-dry as he addressed her.

She reached up to free her bun, then gave a resigned grimace. "Not that you'll care but I interrupted my date to return to the office for this assignment."

"A *date*? With an actual guy?" Heavy skepticism laced his voice as he retrieved my overnight bag.

The woman rolled her eyes and turned to me. After a quick once-over, she held out her hand and smiled. "I'm Maggie, Mr. Steele's long-suffering assistant. You must be Lily Gracen?"

At my nod, her face turned serious. "We'll catch the A-hole who's doing this to you. Don't tell my boss I said so, but he's ace at what he does. Our success record is pretty impressive. You're in good hands."

Caleb slammed the door. "Cut the corporate spiel, Maggie. Lily already knows she can trust me."

I ignored him, and smiled at Maggie. "Thanks."

"Did you bring what I needed?" he asked his assistant.

Maggie nodded. "Everything is already on board."

"Are we cleared to fly?" he pressed impatiently.

"Almost." She pointed to where the copilot was talking to the ground crew. "They're not happy that you're flying outside curfew—"

"You told them it was an emergency, right?"

"Yes, boss. They still need to tick their boxes. Give them a minute."

"I don't have a minute," he snapped, turning toward the group.

"Seriously, they're almost done—" Maggie started, but he was already walking away. She stopped talking, looking a little perplexed.

I frowned. "Is he always—?"

"The definition of a bull in a china shop? Surprisingly, no," Maggie answered her own question, her voice contemplative. "Sure, he's impatient and he wants everything done yesterday, but it takes a lot to ruffle his feathers. Although…"

"Although?" I prompted after a throb of silence, telling myself it was just mild curiosity that triggered the desire to know what made the enigmatic fixer tick. What made him give a damn and what bounced off those impressive shoulders?

Maggie's sharp, gray-eyed gaze snapped to me. I suspected the evasive answer before she opened her mouth. "A testy client earlier tonight before he came to see you. That's all."

I suppressed surprisingly sharp disappointment and glanced over to where the man I'd appointed as my fixer was gesturing impatiently to the men. He stood over a head taller, easily the most striking, and the low timbre of his voice rumbled through the large space, sending a decadent shiver to my lady parts.

After a minute the officials handed over papers to the copilot.

Caleb returned and picked up the overnight bag he'd set down next to the car. "We're clear to fly. Shall we?"

I sidestepped him when he reached for my arm, prompting another raised eyebrow I ignored. The lingering tingle between my thighs insisted touching him was a bad idea.

"Great to meet you, Maggie," I said.

The assistant smiled. "Likewise."

I walked up the stairs to the plane, aware that he trailed behind me. Drawn by an undeniable need, I looked over my shoulder. He'd paused with one foot on the bottom step; his eyes were fixed on me. Or rather on my ass. That insane tingle intensified between my legs.

I barely had time to step back before he was towering over me. For a handful of seconds, he stared down at me. Then his gaze flitted past me to the small cabin.

"Go grab a seat, Lily. We need to be wheels up before the stiffs out there find another reason to delay us."

The interior of the plane was as pristine and classy as the outside. Fitted in mahogany and cream tones, the club seats were grouped into two sections, one side with a shiny table separating the seats and the other without.

I chose the seat with a table. Anything for a buffer between Caleb and myself.

He watched me slide into the window seat. He didn't immediately sit down, even though the jet was rolling out of the hangar. Instead, he took his time to shrug off his lightweight jacket. The midnight blue shirt underneath was fitted, lovingly following a streamlined torso.

When he pivoted to hang up his jacket, the muscles in his back rippled with a sleek, edgy synergy that triggered a need to see him minus that shirt. Unlike me, he was perfectly tanned, the Californian sun having found the ideal specimen to blaze upon. Without a doubt, he would be firmly toned all over.

The urge to glide my fingers over those muscles intensified the incessant throb in my pussy.

I inhaled unsteadily, shifted my gaze and focused on securing my belt as he slid onto the seat opposite me. A moment later one arm extended toward me.

Annoyingly agitated with my skittish emotions, my head jerked up. He was unbuttoning his cuffs, casually folding back his sleeves, exposing thick, brawny arms overlaid with silky wisps of hair.

The innate grace flowing through the moment was almost hypnotic.

God. Enough.

The man was mouthwateringly attractive, granted. But I'd never lost my head or hormones like this, not even during the brief months I thought I was in love with Scott Wyatt, the man Chance planted in my life to manipulate me. Even before I found out his true motivations, Scott didn't set me on fire with a mere look.

After he was done with his hot little arm-porn display, Caleb rested his arms on the table. "Do you want a drink?"

"I'm good, thanks."

He nodded and glanced at his watch. "It is three in the morning, and we land in about forty-five minutes. We can use the time to discuss the case, or you can get some sleep?"

"You're giving me a choice?"

He smiled. "I'm not a complete ogre, Lily, regardless of whatever impression Maggie gave you."

It unsettled me that he'd read me so accurately. But wasn't that why I chose him? He'd risen to the top of my list almost immediately when I searched on the dark web because he was a maverick to the core. Totally unscrupulous when he went after something he truly wanted.

And the way he was staring back at me strongly suggested I was somewhere on his *want* list.

Maybe that was the reason I should've been bone-tired but felt oddly invigorated despite being awake for twenty hours straight. If I'd been coding, I'd be getting ready to crash hard by now.

My stalker's latest "gift" arriving in my mail this morning had wiped rest from my mind.

That unwelcome reminder refocused me. "I'm fine to answer your questions."

His brisk nod signified the switch back to fixer mode. "We'll get to the background stuff when you've had some sleep. For now, tell me when you first realized you'd attracted someone's attention?"

I didn't need to think hard. The memory was etched in my mind. "About seven weeks ago I received a piece of what looked like my code in an email. It was a very rough copy but it got my attention. And no, I wasn't able to find out who sent it."

"So we could be dealing with corporate sabotage."

The possibility shocked me. "You think one of SDM's competitors could be behind this?"

The underhanded tactics that went on in Silicon Valley weren't a secret, but usually they involved throwing enough money at an acquisition to secure it or throwing even more money at a problem to make it go away.

His mouth twisted. "You'd be surprised at the lengths companies would go to get an edge on the market. If your code is as revolutionary as you say it is—"

"It is," I confirmed. The possibilities of my algorithm scared me a little but I was extremely proud of what I'd achieved. The thought of someone stealing it filled me with equal parts fury and fear.

Caleb leaned back but it didn't release me from the raw force field of his personality. I was convinced he'd need to be in another state for that to happen.

"Then I suggest we make a list of the top twenty companies you think might benefit from this code."

I shook my head. "That'll be nearly impossible to investigate before the deadline."

A fierce light blazed in his eyes. "Make the list, Lily. I'll take care of it."

I got the unassailable impression that he would. The depth of that belief scared me a little. But it excited me even more. Which was ludicrous and a lot disturbing considering I detested being taken care of.

Not true. You hate that no one's cared enough without having an ulterior motive. Just like you hate that soft place inside you that wants to be taken care of.

I tightened my gut against the abrading truth. But it was no use. Lately, I hadn't been able to suppress thoughts of my stepfather as easily as I used to. Truth was, my stalker had amplified the yawning cavern of my life. He, or *they*, had exposed vulnerabilities that made me feel raw and fearful and *alone*. It was that last sensation I especially despised. I wanted that aloneness gone, and if I had to endure Caleb Steele for a while to achieve a return to normal, then so be it.

"Okay, I'll have it ready for you in the morning."

"Good. Tell me when you first noticed this wasn't just an online thing?" he whipped back, sharp eyes narrowed.

A swell of fear met quiet fury at the recollection of that first violation. "Two weeks ago I got another piece of code in the mail. It's a long way from the one I was working on, but someone out there is taunting me with knowledge of what I'm working on."

A muscle rippled in his jaw. "Did they make demands? Ask for money?"

"No."

"They're trying to scare you into changing your routine. Trip you up in some way. When was the next time?"

"He left me another code on top of my bike outside a coffee shop four blocks from my house."

His mouth thinned. "So he knows where you work and live."

I fought the shudder that rolled up my body. "Looks like it."

His hands curled into loose fists but his breathing didn't change. He carried on staring at me with a level look, then nodded for me to go on.

"The last time was yesterday morning. I received another code, but with a picture of me attached."

"A picture?" Caleb asked.

I nodded, a sheet of ice unravelling through me at the recollection. "It was taken two days ago. I was shopping."

"Fuck." Caleb's jaw rippled with tension before he leaned forward, bristling with quiet fury. "What happened to the package?"

"I have it at home."

His expression tight, he reached for his phone and had another conversation with the unflappable Maggie, issuing terse instructions about retrieving the package and having a discreet service dust it for prints. Just as briskly, he hung up and dropped the phone on the table between us.

"Tell me about your online activities, outside of the work you do for SDM."

"That's a very broad question." The plane dipped, taking a little bit of my stomach with it. "You want to know if I messed up somewhere?"

"I'm sure you didn't but something you did triggered this."

The logic was too sound to dismiss. I tried to suppress it but my unease grew. "You don't think I covered my tracks?"

A smile twitched his lips. "You're a coder. I'm sure you can clear your caches in your sleep. And I'm not talking about porn. Although I'd love to know which sites you prefer."

A flush heated my chest and spread lower to my abdomen. "Mr. Steele—"

"Lily?" he responded with a heavy dose of snark.

I took a calming breath. "I don't leave a trail of where I buy my lingerie or post minute-by-minute details of where I'm going to be at any given time of day. I know how to protect myself."

"And yet he found you," he stated with bracing finality.

After a moment, I looked at him. "What do you want to know specifically?"

"Coders make decent hackers. If you hacked your way into a job with SDM, you must be great. What's your hacker handle?"

All of a sudden the name that sent shivers down the spines of faceless dark web hackers felt pretentious. "Cipher Q."

His brows slowly rose. "You're Cipher Q?"

Another emotion swept in to mingle with the cocktail swirling inside me. This time it was most definitely not *unpleasant*. "You know about me?"

He shrugged. "Cyber crimes are a problem for a few of my clients. Maggie and a few people on my payroll keep an eye on things like that for me. A few months back she wouldn't shut up about some big-deal hacker contest going on. You won, if I remember correctly?"

The kick of pride warred with the need to set him

straight. "Yes, but it was all aboveboard. No cyber crimes involved."

"Who came second?"

"Nordic Razor."

"What do you know about him? How did he take coming second?"

"You think he's doing this?"

His shoulders rippled beneath his shirt as he shrugged again. "Not everyone likes losing to a woman."

I shook my head. "It's not him."

"I'll be the judge of that. I need the names of everyone who took part in the contest, too."

"At this rate I'll be spending all my time compiling lists for you. I won't have time to work."

He shot forward and the force of his dominant personality hit me like a tidal wave. "You won't be working at all if this situation escalates. Did you forget already that I'm in control here?"

I'm in control.

Words I'd heard far too many times in my life. Words that had imprisoned me for far too long. My teeth met in a grinding clench. "I don't like being ordered around, Mr. Steele."

"Too bad. Until this bastard is in custody, you'll not only do as you're told, you'll also learn to love it."

Maybe it was something in his voice. Or the words he used with me. But my fury faded, along with that carnally needy, traitorous voice that wanted to say, *Yes, Caleb. I'll learn to love it.* That tingle between my thighs still throbbed, but it was with a different sort of need.

A burning need to, for once in my life, grab and

keep the upper hand. To put this man in his place once and for all.

Because, fuck that noise. My days of pretzeling myself to please others were nearly behind me.

I unclipped my seat belt and was out of my seat before I fully processed my actions.

Being pint-size had its advantages. It made crawling on top of the table a piece of cake.

I relished Caleb's unguarded intake of breath as I leaned forward and shoved my face in his. With a couple of inches separating us, I caught every fleck of surprise in his eyes as he watched me.

"You really think you're in control here?" I murmured softly.

A slow, assured smile widened his sexy mouth. "I know it," he rasped.

"I see." I scooted another inch closer, glided my tongue over my bottom lip. His demeanor changed. His ravenous gaze dropped to my mouth and his next breath wasn't quite so steady. "You didn't ask me how I found you to handle my problem, Mr. Steele."

His eyes grew wary. Good. "Maggie handles background stuff."

I nodded. "Hmm. She did ask me the right questions. But I'm afraid I told a little white lie. I don't personally know the client I named as my reference. I found him, and your whole client list, some other way."

A muscle ticked in his jaw. "You hacked me."

I allowed myself a little smile. "No, I *skimmed* you. But you know what I could've done if I wanted to?"

His eyes narrowed. "What?"

"Uncovered every…single…detail about you."

Silence throbbed. The muscle jumped faster. "What's

to stop me from bending you over this table right now, giving you the spanking you richly deserve before I dump you in Palo Alto and walk away?" he breathed through gritted teeth.

The erotic image of his palm turning my ass pink threatened to wipe off my smile. I ignored the balloon of heat dampening my panties and traced my fingers over his jaw, suppressing a gasp at how warm and vibrant he felt.

His sharply exhaled breath washed over my face.

"Because I took a little peek at your active cases. I wanted to make sure I'd be your number one priority. Your most exciting case finished two weeks ago. You're a man of action, and you're bored, Mr. Steele. Right now mine is the juiciest case to drop into your lap."

My thumb skated dangerously close to his lips. He bared his teeth, and another image flashed into my mind—how those perfect whites would feel grazing my clit.

"I could always take the vacation I've been promising myself for a while now," he rasped.

"You won't. Because I also saw the way you looked at me when I walked into the room tonight. The way you're looking at me right now."

My fingers drifted down his solid neck to his collarbone, then over his hard chest to rest on his belt. Without breaking eye contact, I closed the gap between us and brushed my lips, whisper-light, over his, reveling in the instant clutch of lust that darkened his eyes.

"I know you're rock-hard for me, that you've imagined a dozen different positions in which to fuck me."

I drew back and pried my gaze from his to the fists clenched with white-knuckled control on the table on either side of my body. "But you won't touch me, not until you catch my stalker. Because you don't mix business with pleasure. I know that about you, too."

My hand dropped to its final destination, gliding over the stiff, mouthwateringly impressive bulge behind his fly from root to tip. A strangled growl left his throat.

"So, you think you're in charge, Mr. Steele? Dream the fuck on."

CHAPTER FOUR

Caleb

JESUS FUCKING CHRIST.

I stared at her, torn straight down the middle between fury and pleading. Between shoving her ass out of my plane and begging her to stroke my cock again. Harder. Between admitting that yes, she and her case intrigued me, and the urge to say *to hell with it*.

Back in her seat, she stared at me, a saucy smile lifting her delicious mouth. A smile I promised to wipe clean the first opportunity I got.

Shit.

Women with mouths like hers shouldn't be allowed to swear unless there was immediate, no-holds-barred fucking involved. Because between that, the almost-kiss and tortuous stroking of my dick, I was now guaranteed to walk around with a hard-on strong enough to shatter glass.

Even my fury at her invading my privacy wasn't enough to calm the fire raging in my crotch. The knowledge burned, though, along with a need to know what else she found when she went... What did she call it? *Skimming?*

Did she know about my mother's suicide? About the desperate but ultimately fruitless measures I'd used to try to save her? About that one session with the child psychologist after my meltdown? Thankfully, the nightmares that had dogged me since her death weren't on record anywhere.

Still…she'd crossed the line.

Why?

"That was a dangerous little play you staged there, Lily. Is control really that important to you?"

The answer blazed in her eyes before she lowered them. "Isn't it to everybody?" she fired back.

Okay. Control, or giving it up, was an issue for her. I tucked away that piece of info.

But despite her spine of steel, I didn't need to look hard to spot her apprehension. Plus, she was on edge. Clients in that state tended to knee-jerk the hell out of situations.

I took a breath as the plane taxied to the hangar. "You went to a lot of trouble to hire me. Don't fuck it up by digging into my life again. Trust me, I'll know. And I won't give you a pass next time. In return, I'll loop you in as much as I can. Deal?"

She stared at me, the fire raging in her eyes for another second before she offered a curt nod. "Deal."

I rose from my seat, uncaring that my erection still throbbed stiff and eager in my pants.

She'd stoked the fire. She deserved to burn a little. And from the pink staining her cheeks as her beautiful eyes dropped to my crotch, she was burning all right. Still twisting with fury and lust, I leaned down and whispered, "As for your assessment about how many ways I want to fuck you, try a few dozen times north of your calculation. And, guess what?"

Defiant eyes met mine. "What?"

"I know you want me, too, so I guess I won't be the only one suffering, huh?"

She didn't answer, not that I was expecting one.

We both retreated into our thoughts as we exited the plane.

The ride Maggie had organized was a sturdy SUV with darkened windows, which I appreciated. Sadly, there were a million ways for stalkers to spy on their victim these days, and a million ways for victims to respond if they felt powerless.

The thought triggered a question that helped to drag my attention off Lily's small but perfect body and thoughts of what I wanted to do to her. "Do you own a gun?" I asked after stashing our bag and hopping into the driver's seat.

Her eyes widened as she shut her door. "A gun? Why would I own a gun?"

"Don't look so surprised. You'd be shocked by how many people exercise their right to carry a firearm. I don't want to be surprised down the road." I rolled my shoulder as unwelcome thoughts of Kirsten, my ex, and phantom pain from my bullet wound registered.

Lily caught the movement, questions filling her eyes as she replied, "No, I don't own a gun. And I don't intend to arm myself, regardless of this situation."

"Good."

She kept quiet, until curiosity got the better of her. "Were you—?"

"You've pried enough for one night, Lily. Let's focus

on why I'm here, okay?" The snap in my voice made her flinch, but I didn't regret it.

I stuck to a quieter, longer route from the airport to Lily's address in Menlo Park. She started to fidget when we turned into the tree-lined road that housed a row of impressive mansions.

"Will your guys still be there?"

I checked the time on the dashboard. "No. Maggie texted me when they left. They'll come back tomorrow to take care of the security inside the house."

Surprise widened her eyes. "Oh. Thanks."

I glanced over to see her worrying the inside of her lip again. "You're welcome. Wanna tell me why having them inside the house makes you so nervous?"

She averted her gaze. "I'm not comfortable with strangers invading my space," she muttered.

I sensed she wasn't being entirely truthful but let the matter drop. "Okay."

She looked relieved as I checked out our surroundings.

Half of the properties were displayed in all their sprawling glory, but the other half were hidden behind palm and fir trees. Many places for a stalker to hide.

Lily pulled out her phone and hit a button on the screen, nodding at the property coming into view. "It opens the gates."

The electronic gates were swinging open much too slowly. "They need to open faster. You don't want to be a sitting duck out here while the gate takes its sweet time to let you in. I'll get it fixed."

She nodded. "Okay."

When the gap widened, I drove through. Compared to the other houses on the street, hers was on a smaller scale but still impressive enough to blend comfortably into the neighborhood.

Built on two levels with a tapered roof, the tiered white European-style mansion took up several thousand square feet, with tall rectangular paned windows that drew an inward grimace. All her stalker needed was a decent set of binoculars and he could follow her every move when she was home. And that second floor tier was also a problem especially if my suspicion that one or all of the bedrooms came with a terrace overlooking the backyard was confirmed.

The front door looked solid enough, though. I couldn't do anything about the Roman pillars framing the front porch, but the seven-foot potted plants on either side of the door needed to be relocated.

She opened her door and jumped out. I stopped myself from growling my annoyance and got out, reaching her just as she climbed the last step onto the stone-laid porch.

I touched her upper arm. "Wait."

Apprehension flickered across her face. "Your security people were just here. Surely you—?"

"Can't be too careful. Keys?"

She dug through her satchel and handed the keys over. I unlocked the door and saw a large foyer.

"There's a light switch on your left," she said.

I flicked it on, bathing the large space in a warm golden glow. An alarm beeped from a panel next to the switch. I entered the code.

Silence settled in as I took in the layout of the first floor. Two short corridors forked from the entrance foyer on either side of a grand staircase made of wood and trellised iron. At the end of the left hallway, I saw shadowy frames of sofas and a coffee table, which meant the right hallway probably led to the kitchen.

I motioned her inside and turned the dead bolt on the door. "Stay here. I'll check out the other rooms," I murmured. The gun I'd tucked in my back before we left the airport rested reassuringly against my skin.

She sucked in a slow breath before her gaze met mine. "I prefer to come with you," she whispered firmly.

The statement wasn't made out of fear of being on her own. No, Lily was nervous.

The possible reason why hit me with a punch. "Do you live here alone?" I demanded.

"What if I do?" Her chin rose, daring me to have a problem with it.

"Hey, I'm not judging." The size of the house didn't warrant the question. "I'd rather not surprise anyone at four in the morning."

Her gaze swept away. "Oh, right. No, there's no one else here," she murmured.

"Okay, you can come. Just stay behind me, got it?"

She jerked out a nod, albeit a distracted one.

There were no surprises in the kitchen or the pantry, same for the sizeable laundry room. I double-checked the outer doors to make sure they were locked before inspecting the other rooms on my way into the living room.

I guessed the reason for her uneasiness a few minutes later.

The two living rooms connected by a long entryway with a door leading to a study weren't exactly untidy, but they weren't pristine, either.

A discarded throw on one side of the sofa, an empty glass on the table, cushions on the floor in front of a marble fireplace. Over one arm of another sofa, a tank top draped precariously with a black lace bra tucked into the sleeves. Besides the superficial untidiness, all the surfaces were clean, and the decor was tasteful enough to show someone cared enough to make the house a home.

However, when I glanced over, her cheeks were pink, adorable shades of strawberry over the cream.

"So I'm not the tidiest person in the world," she said defensively. "When I'm buried in work I forget to pick up after myself. And I gave my housekeeper time off, so…" She shrugged, then skirted the sofa, her gaze darting furtively around the room.

"You like to be comfortable in your own space. Nothing wrong with that." Except the sight of those plump cushions in front of the pale marble fireplace was restoking the fire she started on the plane.

She snatched the tank and bra off the sofa and dropped them into a cabinet drawer.

I dragged my gaze from her to properly study the room. Two sets of doors led outside. Lots of windows covered by expensive-looking drapes. All to be secured tomorrow.

As if drawn by magnets, my eyes returned to the cushions, to the hint of bright pink poking out from between two cushions. Before I could confirm what it was, Lily moved to block my view of it.

I raised an eyebrow and her color deepened.

"Shall we move on?" she blurted.

I ate the grin threatening, welcoming the chance to cool my raging libido. "By all means."

We retraced our steps to the foyer and headed downstairs to the basement.

A flick of a switch illuminated the corners of the impressive movie theater, equipped with everything a movie buff needed, including luxury loungers and an extensive 1950s-style snack and drinks bar at the far side of the room. I checked out the bar, the small pantry and the bathroom before motioning for her to enter.

She made a beeline for the front row and the object lying out in the open.

The bright pink object was the same as the one I saw upstairs, but this vibrator clearly stood out against the black sheepskin throw discarded on the middle seat facing the giant screen.

My breath locked in my lungs as an image of her spread out on the lounger with her favorite gadget between her legs sideswiped me. Before I could recover from it, another image punched through. This time I was the one positioned between her legs, seeing to her pleasure as whatever chick flick she preferred played in the background.

Only she wouldn't be able to concentrate on a single thing on the screen. Hell, no.

She would be half out of her mind, grabbing my hair and arching her back as she begged me to *please, please, please* get her off.

My pulse kicked into uncomfortable levels as I watched her grip close over the sex toy.

"Can I make a suggestion?" My tongue felt as thick as the hard-on pressing against my fly.

Her fingers clenched around the pink object. "No."

I adjusted myself before moving toward her. "If you're that embarrassed by having anyone see your naughty toys, maybe don't leave them lying around?"

"A gentleman wouldn't mention this," she snapped.

"And a lady wouldn't have crawled onto the table on my plane, teased me with her body and stroked my cock without at least buying me a drink first, but here we are."

"I didn't stroke you…it," she replied hotly. "I just…" Her blush deepened.

I laughed, enjoying her discomfort a little too much. Not so much as the memory of her hands on me because it triggered a craving for more of the same.

"Lily, I don't really care what toys you play with so there's no need to feel bad about it. I am curious about what else you have stashed around the place, though. Personally, I like cold beers in coolers handy around my place but I guess with you it's sex toys? Is it super-efficiency or do you just get crazy impatient when the mood grabs you?"

Sharp, irritated green eyes aimed lasers at me. "I'm going to bed, Mr. Steele. Please take that as a sign that I won't be answering your inappropriate questions." She shot for the door, moving quicker than I anticipated.

I intercepted her before she reached the foyer. "I haven't checked upstairs yet."

"Then I suggest you get on with it." She headed for the stairs.

"Stop." There was more grit in my tone, more pressure in my grip.

"Don't talk to me like I'm Maggie, Mr. Steele," she bit out.

My thumb slid over her skin before I could stop myself. "I would never mistake you for Maggie. You're in a class of your own, sweetheart. And call me Caleb." The gruffness in my voice was a direct testament to what touching her was doing to me.

It had some effect on her, too, if her parted lips and the small gust of breath that escaped was evidence enough. I was completely stumped by the effect of that tiny sound on my dick.

The undercurrents that had swirled around us since we first set eyes on each other strengthened by the minute.

Shit, I needed to cool off before I did something crazy, like drag her close and taste her sinful mouth properly.

"Let's get this over with. Same rule applies: you stay behind me."

After confirming everything was good, I grabbed the bags from the car, fighting the temptation to pour myself a drink. Much as I wasn't looking forward to sleeping under a strange roof, I couldn't compound my rest with alcohol. The nightmares always found a way to filter through anyway.

Teeth clenched, I headed back upstairs.

Maybe choosing the bedroom next to Lily's wasn't the brightest idea. Most nights the nightmares only triggered cold sweats. But there were times when that last image of my mother ripped...*sounds* from me.

I eyed Lily's door. She'd shut it firmly in my face after a curt good-night.

A tight smile tugged at my mouth. She wouldn't appreciate being called a spitfire but that was exactly what she was. Despite the dark clothes and alabaster skin, she blazed red-hot underneath, a fuse ready to explode.

My grip tightened on the doorknob. Was she using her little pink toy right now to take the edge off her irritation with me? To bring much-needed relief from the shadows lurking in the dark?

Fuck, I was in danger of dying from blue balls if I didn't get myself under control.

CHAPTER FIVE

Caleb

It was barely daylight when the ashen image of my mother's lifeless face jerked me from sleep to the pinging of the alarm. I ignored my racing heart as I sprinted for the door and yanked it open, relieved that it wasn't the continual blare announcing a possible intruder. Until I remembered that I was dealing with a tech-savvy stalker.

Downstairs, I took a moment to listen. Only the muted chorus of birdsong broke the silence.

Followed a second later by the faint splash of water. The gun I grabbed from the nightstand before leaving my room bumped against my thigh as I moved toward the open living room door and stepped through it.

Thirty feet away from the back patio, the pristine lawn gave way to stone tiles and a larger-than-average pool.

And right there, swimming without a care in the world, was Lily.

Irritation and disbelief drove me past the large ivy-twined oak pergola with the center fire pit and the loungers that stood to one side of the swimming pool.

My gaze was fixed on the figure weaving through the water, completely oblivious to my presence.

I watched her swim one lap. Then another. I breathed in and out. Slow, deep to get myself under control.

No joy.

"Lily." My voice pulsed with the quiet fury running through my veins.

She didn't stop. Her strokes were flawless and efficient, her strong kicks propelling her swiftly away from me toward the far end of the pool. I trailed after her, watched her execute a neat underwater flip, turn and launch herself into another lap. The move was smooth enough for me to see the wireless swimming earbuds plugged into her ears. My pissed-off barometer ticked up another notch.

I tugged my T-shirt over my head and stepped out of my sweatpants before diving into the pool. Two hard kicks later, she was in front of me. Alarm flared in her eyes as my hands closed on her arms. She fought back, clawing and thrashing the water before she realized who she was fighting.

In that time an unhealthy number of what-if scenarios whizzed through my head, darkening my already foul mood.

"Are you out of your mind?" I made no effort to keep my temper from showing.

She sluiced water out of her eyes with one hand and attempted to push me away with the other. The hell I was budging. "Can you not yell at me, please?"

"I asked you a question."

"Well, you're not going to get an answer if you don't let go of me. Or lower your voice by a couple of thousand decibels."

Fine, so my voice was a little loud. It was barely daylight and I'd slept like shit. "I said—"

"I heard you the first time. I'm pretty sure the neighbors heard you, too." She attempted to break free. I held her tighter, propelling her from the center to the side of the pool.

The water wasn't deep but with her small stature, her feet dangled above the bottom. When she tried to move again, I trapped her with one leg.

She wriggled, braced one hand on my shoulder. The small charge that detonated inside me at her touch was perfectly echoed in her expression. A tiny hitch in her breathing, and then her hand disappeared into the water. "What are you doing?" Her voice squeaked but that fire that was never far from the surface blazed pure challenge with her glare.

I shoved away the effect of her hand on me and glared right back. "I think that's my question. What the hell were you thinking, coming out here on your own?" I demanded.

The first rays of the sun chose that moment to emerge and bathe her face in golden light, illuminating the pearls of moisture dotting her pale, beautiful skin. I couldn't take my eyes off the three fat drops clinging to her top lip. Or the pure temptation of her full lower lip.

"I couldn't sleep. Swimming relaxes me—wait, why am I explaining myself to you?" She shifted impatiently, her toes brushing my bare calf.

I clenched my teeth and tried not to let the heat stabbing my groin distract me. Now that I had her attention, it was probably wise to let her go.

Not until I made my point.

"Do I really need to spell it out to you? And these

things in your ears?" I tugged the earbuds out and tossed them onto the tiles. "How the hell do you expect to hear anything with them plugged in?"

"I always swim with my earbuds in. And no, I can do without that narrow-eyed judgment. This is my home. My life. I can do whatever I want."

"You have a thing for control. Trust me, I get it. But you don't know when this creep will step things up another level. Why the hell didn't you wake me if you wanted to swim so badly?"

She blinked. "I swim every morning, and I don't need your permission to do it."

"For fuck's sake. That's what I'm here for—"

"I'm not going to live in fear and let some random stranger pull my strings!"

The forceful words hit the tranquility of the cool morning. Echoed all around us before settling like a boulder between us. Lily froze as if her outburst had electrified her into silence. The stunned look on her face confirmed she hadn't meant to voice them.

When she went a little pale, I frowned my concern. "Lily—"

"Let me go!"

Her hands rose in the water. One braced on my stomach, the other brushed my upper thigh, then my bare hip. Her green eyes went wide. A moment later her gaze dropped down my chest, and then lower. She gasped. "Are you...*naked*?"

Despite my disgruntlement, I smiled. "I don't get my favorite sweatpants wet for just anyone, sweetheart."

Delicious heat poured into her cheeks as her hands jerked away from my body. "Oh, my God!"

"Why the outrage? Just a few hours ago you were stroking—"

"Shut up!"

I followed the blush, unable to take my eyes off the alluring sight of it. God, I wanted to taste that blush, trail it with my tongue up and down her body.

"My, what a hot little temper you have. I could—"

The words choked off as the hands that pushed me away a minute ago clutched my head and yanked me down to meet her waiting lips.

She kissed me. Then bit me. Hard. Then swallowed my stunned groan into her open mouth as she swiped her tongue over the sting. Once, twice, then with slow, dragging licks that rained fire through my body.

Jesus.

I parted my lips to better taste her. She immediately slid her tongue into my mouth, pressing her velvety lips harder against mine as she licked her way inside the way I wanted to lick her pussy—bold and relentlessly. She nipped the tip of my tongue. I groaned again at the taste of her. She was just like I imagined she would be.

Heaven and hell.

Sin and absolution.

Pleasure and—

She pushed me away as quickly as she'd pulled me close. My stunned brain was still absorbing her spectacular taste when she whirled away, planted her hands on the edge and launched herself out of the pool.

"What the fuck—?" The rush of saliva in my mouth as I watched the water glide off her body was disgraceful enough to make me grimace. Jesus, she was breathtaking.

Her glare didn't hold much power, diluted as it was

by her arousal. "That was to shut you up. Nothing more."

My eager gaze raked her incredible body, took in her erect nipples, the pulse racing at her throat. "You sure about that?"

She looked off to the side. After a minute she balled her hands. "Swimming alone is off the table for now. I'll agree to that."

"Let's make a list so there's no confusion. Five minutes in the kitchen okay with you?"

Her eyes still refused to meet mine. "Fine."

Beneath the water, my cock pumped to full, eager life as the sun rose higher, giving me an even better view of her.

The black one-piece was skimpier than most two-piece suits purely because it was held together by a crisscross of ties designed to draw attention to her impressive curves. I stared my fill while telling myself if my gawking made her uncomfortable then it would be a little payback for what she'd just put me through. But I accepted that my reasons were far baser.

She looked even smaller in her bare feet. God, handling her during sex would be infinitely delightful. She turned away and my gaze dropped to her heart-shaped ass, her shapely legs and the cutest ankles I'd ever seen.

I bit back a groan as my groin kicked hard.

Hell, at this rate, I'd need a cold shower before I could conduct a coherent conversation.

When she reached the lounger and grabbed a towel, I struck out for the far side where I'd dropped my clothes.

I hauled myself out, hoping the cool air would do what the tepid water hadn't been able to achieve, and calm my excitement.

Her sharp intake of breath reached me as I bent to pick up my pants.

Don't turn around. Don't—

I turned and surprised her gaze on my ass. On any given day, I would've tossed out a cocky remark, encouraged her to look her fill if she promised to let me do the same. But we were already in uncharted territory and it'd barely been twelve hours since we met.

Not to mention, there were cameras out here, set up by my team, recording every second of our little show. Set-jawed, I pulled on my pants. First priority after our talk would be to access the security feed and delete that stretch of footage.

She'd disappeared by the time I locked the doors and went into the kitchen. Her coffee machine looked as if it hadn't been touched since it came out of the box. After setting it up, I grabbed two mugs and waited for the machine to do its thing.

She walked in just as the first cup filled. The thin, long-sleeved sweater wasn't temperature-raising in and of itself except it was cropped, exposing a good three inches of her midriff. Paired with black leggings hugging every glorious inch of hip, thigh and legs, it was incredibly potent. I swallowed a groan and busied myself making the second cup. Which took all of ten seconds.

"How do you take your coffee?"

She looked surprised at the offer. "Umm…cream with two sugars and a splash of vanilla."

I found the ingredients, stirred them into her cup and handed it over. "If it sucks, keep it to yourself."

She accepted the coffee, took a careful sip, then blinked. "It's good. Thanks."

I got mine and joined her at the kitchen island. "Why

buy a coffee machine if you don't intend to use it?" I asked just for something to do other than stare at the mouth whose taste was now stuck in my head.

"I didn't buy it. It was here when I moved in, along with most of the furniture." Her reply was the stiff, don't-go-there kind.

I ignored the alarm bells. "How long have you lived here?"

Her face tightened. "Three years."

"And you've only worked for SDM?"

She nodded and leaned her hip against the counter. I forcefully redirected my gaze up to her damp hair, anything not to stare at the silky stretch of bare midriff skin or the luscious curve of her hip.

"So why not a condo nearer to SDM's offices in Sunnyvale?" This part of Silicon Valley was CEO territory, usually favored by those with families.

Her long, sooty lashes swept down. "Accommodation came as part of my signing package and this one was available. It was supposed to be temporary until I found my own place but…it grew on me. When the opportunity came up for me to buy it, I did." She shrugged. "Also saved me time on house-hunting."

The well-rehearsed answer heightened my suspicion that something else was going on here. I left it alone for the moment.

"Besides swimming, what else takes you outside on a day-to-day basis?"

"Nothing I can't live without for the time being."

"Great. So we're agreed that you'll give me a heads-up before you head outside?"

Rebellious green eyes met mine across the granite top. "If it'll stop you from diving naked into my pool, then yes." Impatiently, she set her half-finished coffee on the counter with a snap. "By trapping me in my own home, isn't he winning?"

"You're not trapped. You just won't be doing stuff by yourself for a while. Besides, if he thinks you've got someone else in your life he might show his hand sooner."

She frowned. "Someone in my life?"

I shrugged. "He doesn't know who I am. That'll make him nervous. Enough to show his hand, I'm hoping."

She absorbed the words for several beats. "And if it doesn't?"

I felt my face harden. "Then we'll step up the game, take the fight to him."

My days of sitting around, waiting for things to happen were long behind me. Trusting other people to do the right thing for my mother had cost her the ultimate price. She'd suffered for years until she'd taken the only option she felt available to her, leaving me to deal with the aftermath.

The bitter pill I've swallowed all these years rose to the back of my throat again. Ruthlessly I pushed it back down.

Her gaze dropped for a moment. "The other reason I hired you was because your success rate is one hundred percent. I guess you're good at what you do," she murmured as she toyed with the handle of the mug.

I silenced the cocky bastard inside that wanted to strut at the hidden meaning in her words as she tugged one corner of her lower lip between her teeth. "I have a lot riding on finishing my algorithm," she added.

The admission wasn't an easy one and I admired her a hell of a lot for voicing it. It was probably why I skirted the counter to stand in front of her. Why I tucked my finger under her chin and raised her gaze to mine. "We'll catch the bastard. I promise," I said.

Her nostrils quivered delicately as she took a breath. This close, I could see the faint shadows and fear she was fighting lurking in her eyes. She'd been brave up to this point but the edges of her composure were beginning to unravel. I opened my mouth, to promise fuck knows what, but she stepped back.

"Um, about that kiss…"

The memory of it blazed a path through me. "Yeah?"

"It was out of line. I'm sorry."

"I'm…not."

She stiffened. "What?"

I tossed out an offhand shrug, despite the wide pit of *what-the-fuck-are-you-doing* yawning before me. "Technically, I didn't break my rules. *You* got me hard as fuck on the plane. *You* kissed me in the pool."

Her eyes widened. "And that makes it okay?"

"That makes me…okay with not losing any sleep over it." In fact, the more I thought about it the more I grew okay with it.

"Is that how you usually give yourself a pass?" she asked, her face tightening.

"Since you're the only client I've allowed to…handle me like that, I'll say no."

Lily's mouth dropped open.

My answering smile felt tense as thoughts of Kirsten flared up. With her, I did all the chasing, right into the trap she set for me. Since her, my personal encounters had been kept strictly sexual, with a time limit of no more than two months. I'd discovered that was when nesting behavior began cropping up.

One or two women had called me a cold bastard. I'd learned to live with it. I could probably live with Lily's brand of shutting me up, too, although I was a little unnerved that I was inviting her to smudge the lines. "So if the urge takes you, feel free to go with it."

She gasped. "Are you serious?"

I shrugged.

"Well, it won't," she said briskly. "Are we done here?"

Disappointment cut sharp but I brushed it off. "For now. My team will be here at nine to finish setting up inside. What are your plans for today?"

"I'm going to the office in a couple of hours. It's quieter on the weekend. I get a lot more done there."

"We'll go together."

She nodded and walked over to the sink with her cup. After rinsing it, she bent over to place it in the dishwasher. I ogled her heart-shaped ass for a cock-hardening few seconds before redirecting my gaze.

"I'll have the list ready for you in half an hour," she said as she walked out.

I leaned against the counter after she was gone, willing my hard-on to subside even as I tossed around the rationale I'd given her for bypassing my rules.

Would she take it? Did I really want her to?

Hell, yes!

The powerful need behind the thought propelled me from the kitchen in search of something else to occupy my mind.

For the next hour I explored the two acres attached to the house, assessing possible weak points and compiling a list for the security team to tackle.

In the garage I found a gleaming black single-rider motorcycle with chrome detailing next to a compact

Mini. Both were characteristically diverse, but somehow encompassed Lily Gracen's personality perfectly.

Smiling, I finished the check and returned to the house. I set myself up in the dining room and sent emails to Maggie and the security team. Then I logged on to the security feed, played it through until I reached the moments from the pool.

The cameras displayed shots from different angles, but the one placed in the pergola perfectly captured the moment I reached Lily. It showed the tight expression in both our faces as we talked. Her shock at finding me naked. The moment she pulled my head down for that memorable kiss. The perfect arch of her spine and ass as she rose from the water two feet from me, and my blatant hunger as I stared.

I selected the seven-minute frame and moved my finger to the delete button. Only to pause at the point when she glanced over at me after I came out of the pool. Her gaze didn't linger for more than a few seconds, but the effect of watching her watch me pull on my pants was an extreme turn-on. Like a testosterone-filled sucker, I hit Rewind. Watched the kiss. And again. Until my balls screamed under the pressure I was putting on them. Until my dick roared with the need to fuck.

Hard and fast and rough.

Damn. I wish I hadn't watched it. Lily was an extremely attractive female with a delectable exterior wrapped around a core of steel. Not to mention a healthy sex drive she wasn't shy about satisfying with sex toys.

But despite my weakness for strong, intelligent women, rules were rules. They'd kept me at the top of my game for the best part of a decade.

I shut the laptop and shoved away from the table. My

hand slipped beneath the waistband of my sweatpants and I gave myself a quick, jaw-clenching few strokes before standing up.

I wouldn't touch her while she was my client. But there was nothing stopping me from ensuring the ball was kept front and center in her court.

CHAPTER SIX

Lily

HIS SECURITY TEAM arrived right on schedule.

Three men carrying six large black cases grunted various forms of hello before they went to work.

Ninety minutes later they were done and gone. The setup was state-of-the-art and discreet enough to almost blend into the decor but their presence still felt intrusive.

"How soon do you want to head to the office?" Caleb asked after running me through the security procedures.

I paused halfway up the stairs and turned to face him. He was right behind me, so close I could smell traces of chlorine mingling with his natural body scent, which didn't help my desperate need to forget what happened at the pool.

God, he'd tasted incredible—erotic, intoxicating and potentially addictive. Everything I imagined a real man tasted like. And that was with a kiss I'd surprised him with.

Like on the plane last night, taking control had felt... wonderful. Liberating. I went to sleep craving more of it. I woke to the memory of my hand stroking his thick, hard cock. It was what drove me to the pool to cool off.

Except I'd left it craving more of Caleb.

He was waiting for an answer. And I was staring at his mouth like a horny idiot.

I turned away sharply before that left brow completed its mocking ascent. "I just need to transfer data from my laptop to my office work station. So ten minutes?" I needed to be free of his distracting presence for a few hours. The man brought new meaning to the term *larger than life*.

"Sounds good."

Five minutes later I was standing in my closet, assessing my clothes with a critical eye. The notion that I was taking extra time to dress because of *him* intensified my churning emotions. But the powerful thrill that came from knowing Caleb Steele was attracted to me was unstoppable. It was the kind of power that could go to a woman's head.

But power was corruptible. I should know. Between Chance and my stepfather, they'd used their power over me to control my every move.

It wouldn't be like that between Caleb and me, though. He'd given me the green light. Hell, he'd *urged* me to use my power.

And I'd be lying if I didn't admit I was sorely tempted.

God, you're losing it.

I tugged off my leggings and replaced them with black leather pants. I kept my sweater and usual accessories of leather wrist cuffs and choker but I hesitated before reaching for my favorite red lipstick. It drew attention to my mouth, and made me feel sexy but after this morning, did I want to encourage that around Caleb?

Yes, you do. Maybe, even a little too much...

Frowning, I impatiently reached for the peach lip balm.

The earlier I got to the office, the quicker I could disappear into my work and forget my stalker, and Caleb, existed.

He was waiting at the bottom of the stairs, eyes on his phone when I reached the landing. I hated myself for half hoping he wouldn't look up while my stomach churned in hope that he would. Both wishes were answered when halfway down the stairs his head slowly lifted. His gaze collided with mine before those unnervingly hot eyes swept down my body, all the way to the tips of my heeled boots before conducting a slower return journey.

Hell, he wasn't even hiding the fact that he wanted me anymore. Now he'd told me to come for him, he was granting me unfettered access.

By the time I reached the last step, the simmering heat that hadn't quite dissipated since our pool encounter was stoked into foot-high flames, licking their way up to my nipples and turning them into traitorous points of need that stood out against my thin sweater.

As if he could read my thoughts as easily as he could read my body, his gaze dropped to linger on my breasts, then rose to my face again as his breathing altered.

I'm not sure how long we stood staring at one another.

His phone beeped with an incoming message. His gaze dropped for a second, and then he stared back at me.

"Are you ready?" His voice was gruff.

My head bobbed a nod.

As he turned to open the door, I noticed he'd changed

into dark jeans, a black T-shirt and a dark brown leather jacket. "We'll take the SUV."

I stopped. "I usually go to work by bike but I understand that it's no longer a viable option. So we'll take my car."

"No disrespect to your car, but I prefer not to arrive with leg cramps. And before you say it, no, I won't follow while you drive your car."

"But—"

"Sorry, this is one of those nonnegotiable scenarios we talked about. The safe house is also still an option."

I stalked to the SUV and yanked open the door, worryingly aware this man had the ability to unbalance me with very little effort.

I studied his profile as he started the engine and rolled the large vehicle toward the gates. After he drove through, he flashed me a smile, intensifying the heat blazing through me.

God, had I not stood my ground last night, I would currently be ensconced in a cabin in the middle of nowhere with him.

Mr. if-the-urge-takes-you-feel-free-to-go-with-it.

Erotic thoughts and images bombarded me, enough to keep me silent as he drove toward SDM's Sunnyvale offices.

At the checkpoint, I showed my ID, confirmed that Caleb was with me and directed him to my parking spot.

A curl of pride drifted through me as I saw him read the sign attached to my name—*Junior Vice President—Programming & Coding.* Despite the yoke around my neck in the form of my debt to Chance and my stepfather, I knew I'd earned this position. That I was capable of conquering even bigger mountains. It was what

I intended to do the moment I was free of my twin oppressors.

Caleb's glance showed cool respect.

A knot loosened in my chest. Which in turn made me madder that I'd wanted to see that respect in his eyes. Wanted him to see me through another set of lenses than those of a powerless victim needing help from a fixer.

Throwing the door open, I jumped out.

"Lily, wait—"

I was half a dozen cars away when he caught up with me. "What?"

"You don't rush off and leave me behind. Understood?" he gritted out. He was annoyed, too, but trying to hide it with a fake smile. His fingers slipped around my wrist, his gaze scanning the parking lot before returning to mine. "He could be anywhere, including right here in this parking lot, waiting for an opportunity to strike."

I felt the blood leave my face. His hold tightened momentarily, a gesture of comfort despite his annoyance. "I know it's a pain in the ass but it will become much easier if you accept a few temporary changes."

"Like agreeing for you to become my shadow?"

Annoyance receded to leave a smile that looked more genuine. "I was thinking more like your second skin but I'll settle for shadow."

I tried not to recall the feel of his golden skin against mine and failed miserably. "Okay, can we go now?"

"Sure."

And just like that, he'd gotten his way again. Deciding that keeping score would only mess with my sanity, I headed for my place of work.

SDM's San Francisco offices were shaped like two

bananas facing each other, connected by glass and steel walkways on every floor. The hardware development and tech team took up one building, and the software, programming and coding team took up the other.

I entered the left building and smiled at the guard behind the security desk. "Morning, Charlie."

The stout, middle-aged man smiled back. "Morning, Miss Gracen."

"This is Mr. Steele. He's a…consultant visiting from LA for…a while. Can you sort out a security pass for him?"

Charlie's gaze swung to Caleb before he nodded. "Sure thing."

Caleb handed over his ID for verification, took the pass handed over and studied it with a frown as we headed for the elevator.

"What?"

He leveled his blue-eyed gaze at me. "You're a lousy liar."

Heat rushed into my face and I redirected my attention to the LED floor counter. "I'll take that as a compliment."

From the corner of my eye, I caught his deepening scowl.

"Something else bothering you, Mr. Steele?"

"Charlie suspected I wasn't a consultant, and yet he gave me a security pass anyway. I wasn't searched. Like those rent-a-cops in LA, he would've been useless if I truly wished you harm," he snapped.

I hit the emergency stop button on the elevator, my temper once again bubbling to the surface. "First of all, Charlie is good at his job. The normal procedure for bringing a guest into the building is way more stringent than that. He let a few things slide because *he knows me*. Second, you assume that if you'd been holding a weapon on me I would've folded like a cheap noodle. I can take care of myself. If you don't believe me, try me."

The words were hardly out of my mouth before he lunged for me. Strong hands gripped my waist, lifted me high and pinned me against the wall.

"What the hell?" My voice was a husky mess.

"Okay. Challenge accepted."

I tried to snatch the breath he'd knocked out of me with his action and proximity. All I got was a knee-weakening hit of his intoxicating scent. That and intense deep-blue eyes.

His gaze dropped to my lips. He exhaled, long and deep, still staring at my mouth for breath-stealing seconds. His grip tightened around my waist, imprinting heat from his touch directly onto my skin. A low, insistent throb started between my legs.

I dropped my satchel and brought one knee up, only to have him block me with a smooth deflection a few inches before it made contact between his legs. His low laugh made me see red. I slammed both wrists against his neck. The gleam in his eyes mocked me and I knew he could've evaded me if he'd wanted to. But with the semi-blunt spikes from my cuffs digging into his carotid, he was going nowhere.

His thumbs pressed into my hipbones, his body pinning me harder into the wall. "And here I thought those cuffs were just to drive up a man's blood pressure," he breathed against my lips.

The ends of his hair teased my fingers, sparking a need to twist them into his hair. "You can't really be talking since I've just virtually ripped your throat out," I murmured.

He gave another laugh. "True. Score one to you."

"Great. You can…let me go now." Why did the second part of that sentence stick in my throat?

He shook his head. "Not until you agree to stop calling me Mr. Steele."

"And if I don't?" I challenged.

"Technically, I'm dying. I deserve a last wish, don't you think?"

"And your last wish is for me to say your name?"

His gaze dropped to devour my mouth. "Yeah. But I wouldn't mind another taste of you, too. Or those hot little hands on my cock again. Hell, I'll take whatever you give."

"You… I…"

"Ball's in your court, baby," he encouraged thickly, then flexed his hips, offering the vivid imprint of his cock between my thighs as he gave a strained laugh. "Literally."

Dear God. He was thick. And long.

The ache between my legs intensified a thousand times, plumping my clit as my pussy clenched hungrily. I tunneled my fingers through his hair, then grabbed a handful, exerting a little force as I hooked my legs around his waist.

His chest vibrated with a smothered growl as he planted himself more firmly between my thighs. The layers of clothing between us were all but nonexistent as he pressed the solid rod of his cock against my sex.

"Fuck," he groaned. "Your hot little pussy feels so good against my cock."

I lowered my head until our lips were millimeters

apart. Then I slowly undulated my hips, deepening the friction.

"Shit," he growled, his gaze darting between my mouth and where we were pressed together below the waist.

"You like that…Mr. Steele?" I drew my hips back up, nice and slow.

His jaw clenched tight and a shudder powered through him. "You teasing little witch. You'd like nothing better than to see me come right here, wouldn't you?" he muttered.

I wanted him to lose a little control, but not with the bothersome layers of clothes between us. I wasn't going to tell him that, though. "Would you die happy, then?"

"Not even close," he hissed. "Not when I'd rather have you, hot and wet and tight around my—"

"Hello? Is everything okay in there?" A disembodied voice asked from the panel on the elevator wall.

Caleb's jaw flexed, and he swore under his breath. "We're fine," he growled without taking his eyes off me.

"You sure? We have a technician here if you need help?" the helpful voice offered.

"Let me go," I muttered against his lips.

For a charged moment he resisted. Then his grip loosened and he allowed me to slide down the wall. With every inch, the heat of his erection singed me, announced its potency in a way that made my nipples sting and my pussy wetter.

It was ten kinds of inappropriate but for the life of me, I couldn't summon an ounce of regret. All I could think about was what it would feel like to have that thickness *inside* me.

"To be continued, I hope," he murmured against my cheek as my feet met the floor.

He took a step back. Then another. Reluctantly, his hands dropped. Then, without taking his eyes off me, he stabbed the button that released the elevator.

The small rattle before the carriage continued its journey restored some sanity. But even then a large part of me was suspended in disbelief at what I'd done.

Sex with Scott—before I found out that Chance had planted him in my life to control and spy on me—had been lukewarm at best.

What happened to my body when it was within touching distance of Caleb was nothing short of stupefying.

I avoided looking at him as I led us through the open plan space that led to my corner office. Like most tech companies in Silicon Valley, the space was designed to invite easy lounging with the aim of sparking ideas through socializing.

I entered my office, set my satchel down and fired up my three monitors. From the corner of my eye, I saw Caleb checking out the area before refocusing on me.

When he started walking toward me, I reached into my satchel. "Here's the list you asked for."

His hot gaze lingered on my face and mouth for a few ferocious moments before he took the piece of paper. "Thanks."

"If you need somewhere to work, there's a spare desk and computer next door."

He reached into his jacket and I forced myself not to ogle the way his T-shirt stretched across his torso. "No, thanks. This is all I need." He waved his phone at me.

He walked across the room, dropped onto the sectional sofa next to the wall and propped one foot on the coffee table. A minute later his fingers were flying over the keyboard.

I greatly resented the fifteen teeth-grinding minutes it took for me to focus, but eventually I was back in the groove. I spent the next few hours going over the tweaks I'd made that morning.

The snags my coding had hit were frustrating, but I couldn't rush this or SDM would miss the first major beta-testing deadline.

Not gonna happen.

My burning need to be done with Chance depended on everything going smoothly.

There were times I wished I hadn't hacked him. Times I wished I'd called his bluff when he'd turned up at my house with a patrol car and threatened me with jail unless I did what he—and my opportunity-grabbing stepfather—wanted.

Thoughts of how easily Stephen Gracen had thrown his own stepdaughter under the bus slashed painfully through me.

I was stealthily breathing my way through it when Miranda, my assistant, entered.

Her gaze swung to Caleb. And stayed.

His head snapped up, but the laser-eyed scrutiny he'd given my other employees was nowhere in sight. Instead, a slow smile broke over his face as he stared at my tall, attractive assistant.

"Hi," he drawled, slowly rising to his feet.

Miranda's toothpaste-white smile lit up her face. "Hi, I'm Miranda." She strode to him, her hand outstretched. "And you are?"

He took her hand. "Caleb."

"Caleb. Hi," she repeated. Then just stood staring up at him.

I slowly disengaged my clenched jaw. Cleared my throat. They both looked at me.

I opened my mouth to explain Caleb's presence, then remembered his gibe about me being a lousy liar. When his eyebrow started to creep up, I redirected my attention to Miranda. "I wasn't expecting you in today."

She reluctantly dropped Caleb's hand, but I noticed a pronounced sway in her hips as she crossed to my desk. "It was either go off-road biking with the guys from design or finish the assignment you gave me on Wednesday."

"It could've waited till Monday," I replied. Her work had nothing to do with my secret project but she had an aptitude for programming that I utilized when necessary.

She shrugged. "Programming beats the risk of a broken arm, no matter how exhilarating the boys claim biking can be." She glided a hand over her sweater dress and glanced at Caleb. "I prefer a different type of excitement."

He slid his phone into his back pocket and crossed his arms, and I swore Miranda groaned under her breath.

"I'll let you get on with it, then." I couldn't help the irritation filtering through my voice.

She nodded, then flicked Caleb one last glance. "See you around?"

Caleb smiled. "I'm sure you will."

To his credit, or more likely because he knew he could have her if he wanted, he didn't watch her sashay to the door. Instead, he turned his blue gaze on me.

Oh, hell no. I wasn't about to answer questions about Miranda.

The tall brunette could double as a supermodel any day of the week, and was constantly hit on outside the office.

And technically, she didn't fall under Caleb's no-dating-clients rule.

I fixed my gaze on my screen and continued working.

He got the message and returned to the sofa.

An hour later his shadow fell across my desk.

The breath I sucked in didn't quite catch. Irritated by my body's continued betrayal, I raised my head. "Can I help you?"

His mouth twisted in a parody of a smile. "You seem different. Much less…tense." He snapped his fingers. "That's it. You look relaxed."

I cursed the flush that crawled up my neck. "I don't know what you're talking about."

"Sure you do. You're in your element."

"Is this conversation going anywhere? I have a ton of work—"

My breath rushed out when he leaned across the desk and drifted a finger down my cheek. "You really don't need to be so jumpy around me. You especially don't need to get defensive every time I give you a compliment."

"I wasn't—"

"You want to pretend you're offended because I said you're more at home here with your computers than in that gilded cage you call a home. But you don't have to be."

The accuracy of his words made me jerk away from his touch.

My house was luxurious on many levels. But there was more to what I'd told Caleb last night. Truth was, it was also my cage. Chance had stashed me there when I'd first arrived in San Francisco because he'd wanted me isolated. *Still* wanted me isolated. For now it was a place to eat and sleep but it would never be my home.

Caleb was watching me closely, reading my every expression.

My gaze dropped to his throat as I cleared mine. "I'm not. You're mistaken."

He sighed. "What's your favorite restaurant?"

I blinked. "What?"

"Food. Lunch. Where?"

"Why?"

"Jesus. You love making me sweat, don't you, Lily?"

My fingers curled around the edge of my desk, unable to stop myself from replaying those moments in the elevator. The feel of his cock between my legs, his strained voice as he whispered his wishes to me.

All that power and glory under my control...

He leaned closer, sunlight glinting off his dark, mahogany-tipped hair. "What's going through that mind of yours, I wonder?"

I dragged my gaze from his body and named the Japanese restaurant I liked. He tapped it into his phone and I heard a whoosh of a text.

"Why do we need to go out at all? This place has a takeout service. We could just order in."

He shook his head. "Like I said, it's time to change things up a little. Your stalker knows your routines so let's introduce a new element into the equation."

"Let me guess? You?"

"Yep. We're putting ourselves out there. Besides, I

have questions about the people on the list you gave me. I prefer we do it somewhere we won't be interrupted." He jerked his head to where a couple of analysts conversed outside my office. One of them looked up and started to wave.

Caleb's glower froze it dead. They quickly dispersed.

"Wow, you must be very proud of yourself," I said.

He turned back. "Last night you told me what you're working on is top secret."

"It is."

He indicated the clear glass windows. "I would've thought you'd be locked away in a basement somewhere in one of those Faraday Cages."

I opened my mouth, closed it again and tapped a command to shut down my laptop.

"Come on. I'll show you how it works. Then maybe you'll stop glaring at everyone who comes into my office."

He smirked. "I can't make that promise. And I didn't glare at *everyone*."

No. Miranda got the full effect of his megawatt smile. I didn't want to examine why that bothered me so much.

In the elevator, I made sure to keep a distance between us although I didn't escape the sizzling heat of his gaze as he lounged against the opposite wall.

Damn, I'd probably never ride an elevator again without thinking about Caleb Steele.

The code I inputted dropped us down to Basement Level 3. The guard outside the elevator took Caleb's electronic gadgets. We walked down a corridor to a silver metallic door.

"To answer your question, both buildings are equipped with specialist reflective glass that makes it hard to spy on monitors from outside. And then there's this." I led him into a warehouse-size room completely empty except for the large meshed structure in its center with a desk and one chair.

"The Faraday Cage," Caleb muttered.

I nodded.

"What's that?" He nodded to the pedestal set up against the left wall with a small laptop built into it.

"Every keystroke I make on my laptop or work station upstairs is immediately saved into that laptop. Every twenty-four hours, I transfer data from the laptop to the supercomputer in the cage. Hacking it isn't impossible, but it'll be very difficult. And I didn't come down here to work because as you can see there's only room for one down here." I didn't want him prowling outside the cage, like a predator wolf, disturbing me with his presence.

Caleb walked around the cage, examined every inch of the space before returning to where I stood.

"You designed all this?"

I licked my top lip. "Yes."

His gaze heated up, his eyes telling me he wanted to touch me and do other intensely filthy things to me. Things forbidden by his rule. "All that beauty and brains in this killer little package."

That darned swell of pride rose again, mingling with the sizzling fires his eyes evoked in me. "Is that your way of saying you're impressed?"

"It's my way of saying I'm *very* impressed."

Before I could stop myself, I was smiling, shamelessly basking in his praise.

His eyes dropped to linger on my mouth, and his nostrils pinched a little as he inhaled. "You have a beautiful smile, Lily. You should use it more often."

I knew Caleb was attracted to me, but the look in his eyes as he called me *beautiful* shook loose something mildly disquieting inside me.

Just shut up and enjoy the moment.

Except I was enjoying too much of it altogether.

I was paying him to be here. Once his job was done, this would be a distant memory.

Unless you make it infinitely memorable?

I turned away sharply, the potency of that temptation taking me by surprise. Under the guise of taking the laptop to the Faraday Cage to transfer my latest work, I couldn't stop thinking about the possibilities.

Caleb and me.

Doing the dirty.

Last night he'd given me the green light. This morning in the elevator, he'd all but begged me to third-base him.

What was stopping me?

The discovery that Scott was just a pawn strategically placed in my life and not just a guy I'd met at a party and subsequently dated had left a huge deficit in my trust bank, not to mention a gaping vacancy in my sex life. This might be my chance to balance the sex part without the messiness of wondering about authentic emotions.

Plus, if our three brief encounters were an indication, the sex would be off the charts.

"Lily."

God, that voice. Would he sound like that when he was deep inside me, pounding my brains out?

"Lily?"

I snatched in a breath, schooled my expression and turned. "Yes?"

"You done?" he asked with a raised eyebrow.

"Uh-huh."

"Good. Time for lunch."

As we entered the elevator, I remembered other fragments of our conversation upstairs. "You said you had questions."

He was watching me with hooded eyes as if he knew the thoughts running through my head. "Yeah," he replied absently.

"What kinds of questions?" I asked.

He slid his hands into his back pockets. "Different kinds. Personal and professional. Wanna start with the personal?"

My breath caught. "I—"

"Great. When was the last time you had sex?"

CHAPTER SEVEN

Caleb

"YOU'RE GOING TO have to answer me sometime."

After a sharp intake of breath and a furious blush, which took all my severely tested control not to trace with my fingers, she'd clammed up.

To be fair, having a couple of SDM employees join us in the elevator had put the brakes on that conversation.

But she'd maintained silence in the SUV and all the way to the restaurant.

I parked in front of the Japanese restaurant, ignoring the valet waiting for us to exit the vehicle.

"I'm happy to repeat the question if you want? Sex, Lily. When—?"

"I heard you the first time," she snapped, puffing out an annoyed breath as she reached for the door.

I stepped out, a little annoyed with myself, too. Truth be told, I didn't intend to ask her that. Not immediately.

But as suspected, with every revelation of her brilliance, I grew more attracted to Lily Gracen. I'd come within a whisker of calling bullshit on my own rules and kissing her in the Faraday Cage room. After that little cock-teasing incident in the elevator, who the hell would've blamed me? Shit, I was getting hard just thinking about the way she'd worked me between her legs.

And yes, I was a little peeved that she managed to get herself under control before I did. All the same, this was a subject that needed addressing, so why the hell not?

I made eye contact with the two-man security team I had Maggie send ahead, and escorted Lily into the restaurant. The waiter showed us to the private booth I requested.

"Lily." Maggie called this my rumbling volcano voice. "This will go a lot faster if you didn't stop to dissect every question or take offense at it."

She barely blinked at my don't-fuck-with-me tone, studied the menu for a minute before she closed it with a snap. "What has sex got to do with anything?" she hissed.

I shrugged. "Maybe nothing. Maybe everything. I thought you were in a hurry for this to be over?"

"I am, but—"

"How old are you?" It was another pertinent question I hadn't yet asked. She was over the age of consent but the flashes of innocence I spotted every now and then demanded investigation.

"Twenty-four," she answered with a frown. "How old are *you*?" she tossed back.

If she didn't know then she'd told the truth about skimming my past. That put a plus tick in her favor.

"I'm asking the questions here, but if it'll make you cooperate, I'm twenty-nine. I'm six-foot-four. I have all my own hair and teeth. Oh, and I'm single."

A hungry little expression flitted across her face but she hid it well. "How long have you been a fixer?" she returned.

"You must have missed what I just said about questions."

"I'm supposed to trust you with my safety. I deserve to know a little bit about you, don't you think?"

Fair point. In her shoes, I would have a few hundred questions, too. She wasn't a blind follower. Another turn-on. Still... "You get three questions. *After* you answer all of mine."

That earned me a sarcastically raised eyebrow that somehow managed to connect straight to my cock. Fuck.

"What's your deal with SDM? You said you had history," I said.

Her face immediately shuttered. "They put me through college and hired me straight after."

Interesting. "And college was?"

"MIT."

"You're from the East originally?"

The waiter arrived at our table. Lily ordered a soda and six bite-size platters of assorted dishes without consulting the menu.

"I'll have what she's having but with a beer," I said.

The waiter nodded and hurried away.

"Why does it matter whether I'm from the East or not?" she asked warily.

"Is that one of your questions for me?"

"It's a query generated by the fact that I think you're wasting time on pointless questions."

She was unsettled by my line of questioning. Which triggered a need to know more. "You're being stalked, Lily. You don't think details of your background will inform me as to who is after you?"

Her shoulders slumped a little but in direct contrast,

her chin angled up. "Fine, I grew up in Maine, but we moved to Boston when I was ten."

"We?"

"My stepdad and I. And before you ask, neither of my biological parents are in the picture. They haven't been for a very long time."

I crunched on that piece of information for a minute. I wanted details but sensed it wasn't an easy subject, so I dropped it. I had ways to find that out on my own anyway.

"You have a boyfriend?" Living alone didn't mean she wasn't seeing anyone.

Her mouth—her very fuckable mouth—compressed but I spotted the flicker of anguished fury in her eyes. The kind that came from a nasty betrayal. "No. I don't have a boyfriend. If I did, I wouldn't—" She stopped short.

"What? Have sex toys?" I shrugged. "That could indicate a voracious appetite, not the absence of a sex life. Although I'm guessing you're not the kind of girl to wrap your legs around a man's waist and rub your pussy so beautifully against his cock if you belonged to another?"

"God, you're unbelievable," she said under her breath.

"I'm plain-speaking. There's a difference, sweetheart." Mixed signals led to complications. After Kirsten, I wasn't prepared to take that risk.

"When was your last relationship, casual or otherwise?" I pressed. It was obvious I would need to pry every piece of info from her.

Her gaze dropped, and she toyed with the tableware. "Eight months ago."

"How long were you together?" *Where did you meet? I hope he was a lousy kisser and even worse in bed.*

Jesus, Caleb. Get a fucking grip.

"Six months."

Not long by any stretch, but long enough for me to be mildly jealous at the thought of some guy having a claim on her.

The waiter's arrival gave me a moment to examine that jealousy, grimace with disgust at myself for sticking steadfastly to my second and third rules.

I watched her pick up a roll of sushi with her chopsticks and dip it in teriyaki sauce. I did the same and we ate in silence for a while.

"Who ended the relationship?"

She froze. I couldn't stop myself from staring at her glistening mouth, wondering how it would feel when I slid my cock between her lips.

I looked up. She was staring at me. Her cheeks heated up as she accurately read my thoughts.

"Answer the question, Lily."

She dropped her chopsticks, her face tightening again. "I did. And you're wasting your time with this. Scott isn't the one doing this."

"I'll be the judge of that—"

"No! I know what I'm talking about so please drop it," she hissed.

"Not until you tell me why any guy whose veins aren't filled with ice water would quietly walk away from you?"

Her lashes swept down for a moment, then rose again, a challenging fire in her eyes. "Not every guy I come into contact with is a potential stalker."

"Scott wasn't just any guy, though, was he? What aren't you telling me, Lily?"

She remained silent for a long stretch. And I waited her out, biting down my impatience.

"Because Scott wasn't just a guy I met at a party. Chance paid him to seek me out."

Shock bolted up my spine. "What? Why?"

She swallowed and her hands balled into small fists. When she lifted her gaze her beautiful green eyes were far too haunted. "Because he wanted...*wants* to control me."

Jesus. "Again, why?"

"What does it matter?" she snapped. "All you need to know is SDM and Chance need this algorithm. It'd be absurd for him to jeopardize it by having someone stalk me, so just...just take my word for it that it's not Scott, okay?"

I didn't voice the world's worst cliché right then because I didn't want to piss her off even more, or sound like a hormone-addled teenager but, fuck me, she was so incredibly gorgeous when she was mad I lost the ability to think clearly for a minute.

I let her take the deep breaths she needed to calm down.

"You slip into Bostonian when you're agitated, you know that? It's cute."

She looked adorably nonplussed before she shook her head. "Nothing about any of this is *cute*, Mr. Steele."

"I disagree. I wonder, do you sound like that during sex, too?"

Green eyes snapped fire at me. "You'll *never* find out."

I couldn't help myself. I had to touch her again. I reached out and traced the curve of her lower lip with my finger. Soft. Firm. Satin-smooth. "Are you sure about that, Lily?"

She inhaled sharply and her eyes turned a shade darker. "Can we not turn everything into a sexual tennis match? It's really exhausting."

Reluctantly, I retreated. "Has there been anyone else since Scott?"

She picked up her chopsticks again. "Someone briefly. Nothing serious."

"Who, and for how long?"

She sighed. "Mark Callen. For two months. He bought me a coffee at where I get my breakfast. I… I wanted to make sure Chance wasn't still interfering in my life."

My jaw gritted. "Was he?"

She shook her head.

I relaxed a little. "Did you sleep with him?"

Her glare burned me but I didn't let up.

"No," she answered eventually.

I was swimming in relief when she took a sip of her soda. I watched her throat move, wondering why the hell I found that so sexy.

Hell, was anything about her not sexy?

Yeah, the way she kept snippets of information from me. That didn't turn me on even a little.

That Chance thing really pissed me off, though. I made a note to have the asshole checked out.

As for Lily, I wanted to know everything about her. Lily Gracen fascinated me the way no other woman had.

"So you went out with him for two months but didn't sleep with him. What the hell did you do? Hold hands and read each other poetry by candlelight?" I asked.

"So what if we did?" she lobbed straight back.

"Then I'd say it's great you dumped the dickless wonder. You deserve way better than that."

"God, you really are a Neanderthal, aren't you?" she snapped before pushing her plate away. Apparently, we were done eating.

"No, I'm a man with basic but fundamental needs. If I have to endure the R word, then I sure as hell expect some regular fucking as part of the bargain. Otherwise, what's the point?"

"So sex has to be a guarantee in a *relationship* or you're out?"

I took in her white-blond hair and the choker around her neck that howled at me like a damn siren call. The semi-erection that flared to life if she so much as breathed in my direction thickened behind my fly. "I like sex. It's the single decent thing the good Lord granted humanity. I feel zero guilt for loving it. So yes, sex is a hell of a priority for me."

Fresh heat flared in her cheeks, but she still delivered the most dick-torturing smile I'd ever seen. "Except when it comes to your clients, though, right, Mr. Steele?"

Dammit. She was too fucking much. I breached the gap between us, spiked my fingers into her hair and tightened my fist.

She glared at me but didn't struggle to get away. "I'm beginning to think you enjoy taunting me by refusing to use my name," I breathed.

"I don't have a problem with saying your name."

I tugged her even closer. "Then do it."

She looked me straight in the eyes, her tongue darting out to moisten her lips. "Caleb."

I tilted her head until she had no choice but to raise

that gorgeous face, offer up those luscious lips to me. "Again."

She glared fiercer at my instruction, then parted her lips. "Caleb."

The soft, whispered delivery was deliberately provocative. I knew it. But it still chopped me off at the knees. "Fuck." With a groan, I lowered my head, but stopped a breath from her lips. "Kiss me, Lily."

"Why?" she breathed defiantly even as her eyes devoured my mouth.

"Because you're *dying* to. Take it, baby. Take what you want."

Her ragged moan was music to my ears but hell for my cock. All the same, I let go of her, put the power in her hands and nearly roared with triumph as she leaped on me.

And goddamn it all to hell if she didn't taste twice as heady, twice as decadent, as before.

It started with one hot little sound under her breath as my teeth grazed her bottom lip. A cross between a whimper and a sigh, it snaked down my groin, curled itself around my cock and stroked me into rigid life. And that was before I'd even tasted her properly. I nipped her again, resisting the urge to take a deeper, more satisfying bite.

The promise of more lay within, but I was more than content, for now, to just sample her plush lips. Over and over. To hear the tiny sounds turn into moans, to feel her strain toward me as her own hunger clawed at her.

Her hands delved beneath my jacket, clawed at my T-shirt before she slipped them underneath.

In that moment I stopped caring that we were in a public place.

A breath I didn't remember holding expelled from me as her small nails dug into my skin. I suppressed a growl and fought the need to ravage, reminding myself that besides every shitty thing happening in her life, she hadn't had sex in a while. Exhibiting even a fraction of the wild craving whipping through me might send her into retreat mode, and fuck if I was going to allow that to happen.

But God, she was exquisite. The way her lips clung to mine was driving me insane.

"Jesus, you taste amazing." I couldn't help the words from spilling out when we broke apart to get a hit of oxygen.

She tensed. I sucked her bottom lip into my mouth and trailed my tongue over her velvety skin. A sigh and a moan rewarded my effort.

I'll stop in a minute.

We hadn't finished our talk. Plus, we needed to put on the brakes before we were thrown out for public indecency.

Besides, I couldn't sustain this much longer. Not without throwing my rules out the window, flattening her to the booth seat and delivering on every single promise and filthy fantasy I'd harbored since she walked into my life.

But I *could* drag her a touch closer. I *could* slide one hand down her back and mould it around her pert little ass, reconfirm that her flesh was as tight and supple as I imagined.

I would stop. Right after she gave me another of those exceptionally indecent moans.

CHAPTER EIGHT

Lily

HOLY. SHIT.

What the hell was happening to me? Why did Caleb only need to crook his finger before I threw common sense out the window and jumped him?

And these sounds I was making? Yeah, I *really* needed to stop moaning like a whore in church. But up until a minute ago, he'd let me take the lead in our little make-out session.

Then something flipped.

Now, the way he was using his mouth, his tongue, heck, his teeth? In the few times I let him kiss me, Mark's teeth always managed to collide with mine, generating an unpleasant nails-on-a-chalkboard sensation.

Caleb knew how to use his. Little nips at the corner of my mouth that shot fire straight between my legs, even bites on the very tip of my tongue where I had no clue I was so sensitive.

Our previous encounters, I'd felt like I'd plugged into a steady current. *This* was probably what it felt like to bungee jump off a helicopter over a live volcano after being injected with pure adrenaline.

Three numbskulls from the research department confessed to doing that once for the intense rush. I still believed they were completely insane, but if what they experienced was remotely close to what I was feeling now, then…yeah…I got why they would chase such a thrill.

Caleb's tongue swiped between my lips, instantly igniting a yearning to feel it swiping between my legs on its way to concentrate on my clit, now throbbing insistently.

And God, his hand was kneading my ass in that superhot way again.

His hand slipped lower to the curve of my butt and nudged me closer until somehow, I was in his lap. Was that the slow grind of the thick erection against my thigh? Holy…God. He felt even bigger than this morning in the elevator.

The thought of all that power and girth inside me freaked me out a little. Okay, a *lot*.

Until I reminded myself that I had the power. I could stop anytime I wanted. By simply pulling back. Letting go.

Let go!

I dragged my hand down from where it'd ended up on his ripped chest. Down to his waist, to the solid square of his belt buckle. Any lower and I would touch his cock again. I moaned at the intense urge to do just that.

Then I heard the faint clink of cutlery.

We were in a restaurant. In a private booth, yes, but still a public place. And for the third time since I woke up, I was sucking face with the man I'd hired to find my stalker.

Oh, God.

Maybe that adrenaline kick I imagined had really been a hormone shot? Because the sensations racing through my body all craved one thing—Caleb's cock inside me.

I scurried backward from the hot body and the erection digging into my thigh. One hand was still buried in my hair, imprisoning me as he stared down at me with fiery eyes that promised as much filthy fucking as his lips had pledged.

"Lily." His voice was thick. He cleared his throat and swallowed.

Those few precious seconds helped me put more daylight between us. I grabbed his wrists and tugged his hands from my body. He dropped them but not his searing gaze.

I busied myself by picking up my glass of soda and taking a sip I prayed wouldn't choke me. Thankfully, it went down smoothly, cool enough to restore a tiny bit of sanity. "So, you think this little display helped?"

His eyes narrowed. "What?" He shifted away and dropped one hand into his lap. I forced myself not to watch him adjust the bulge behind his fly.

"My stalker. If he's watching. You think it helped or was it all a waste of time?" I forced out as I smoothed my hands over my hair. My scalp still tingled deliciously from when he'd grabbed and pulled my hair. Did he do that during sex, too? I slammed my thighs together before the image of him doing that added to the fire scorching my pussy.

He exhaled sharply. "That wasn't why you kissed me and you know it."

"Do I?" I challenged because, *dammit*, I was out of sorts in more ways than one, and this seesawing from being in total control to losing it around him was driving me nuts.

His eyes gentled. "You don't need to panic, Lily. I'm not going to use this against you. That's what you're afraid of, isn't it?"

My breath shuddered out as panic flared. "Stop talking as if you know me. You don't!"

"I know that control is important to you. Is it because of what your asshole boss did? I'd be wary, too—"

"Tell me why you're so hung up on *your* rules. Is it because of what a *client* did to you?" I lashed out, terrified of how effortlessly he was probing beneath my skin.

A muscle rippled in his jaw. "We're not talking about me."

I forced a laugh. "That tells me everything. Who was she?" I pressed.

His whole face grew taut. "Nobody you need to concern yourself with," he bit out.

The confirmation that someone somewhere had affected him enough to drive his guard up hit me with unnerving disquiet. Nearly as much as his accurate divining of my panic.

"Fine. Can we leave now?" I cringed at the stress in my voice.

He inhaled slow and deep, and then pulled out his wallet.

"I have an account here. They'll put it on my tab," I said.

He scowled as he placed a couple of hundred dollar bills on the table. "I brought you to lunch. I'm paying."

Outside, the brilliant sunlight reminded me it was still daytime. That I had many more hours of work ahead of me.

About to get in the SUV, I caught Caleb scanning the street, his gaze alert. I knew he had men out there but the fact that he was in fixer/protector mode despite the turbulence between us shook loose something I hadn't felt in a long time.

Warmth.

The memory of it was ephemeral—the contented seven-year-old tucked in her mother's arms with no clue that a mother's love could be temporary like everything else.

You're truly losing it.

I slammed the door and shook my head.

Like the outbound journey, neither of us spoke as we drove back to SDM but I knew I had to say something as he pulled up into my parking space.

I undid my seat belt, faced him and opened my mouth. He grabbed me and pulled me across the center console.

"I know it's insane, and we'll both probably regret it, but fuck, I need to kiss you again," he breathed roughly against my mouth.

Before I could take a breath, his tongue slid into my mouth. Wet and insistent and carnal. It was the dirtiest promise of sex I'd ever known. Over and above every inappropriate sexual thing he'd said to me since we met, it was that decadent slide of his tongue against mine that did me in. My hands returned to dig into his waist, my torso straining across the small space to slide against his.

He banded one hand around my waist and lifted me over to his side. And just like that the heat of his cock was a living thing against my ass, announcing its insistent virility. I moaned, half-ashamed at how easily

I'd fallen into the kiss, half-fearful of his sensual power over me.

Slowly, that fear built, insidiously reminding me that this was no longer my default setting. I was so close to true freedom for the first time in my life. I couldn't become a slave to my hormones or my emotions.

I pushed at Caleb's chest before the hand sneaking up my waist could cup my breast. "Stop!"

He froze immediately.

I took a breath. "Let me go."

He stared at me for a full minute, his chest rising and falling in harsh pants. Then his hands dropped from my body.

I hopped over into my seat, struggling with my own breathing.

"Jesus," he swore under his breath, slammed his head against the headrest and closed his eyes. After tense seconds he opened them. "I'm…" He stopped and gritted his teeth. "Hell, I suppose you want an apology?" Before I could answer, he continued, "You're not going to get one because I'm not sorry. You, with that tight, gorgeous body and that bruised, ripe mouth, are fucking irresistible," he growled.

My lungs deflated in a giddy rush. Heat spiked through my blood, and my panties grew shamelessly damper. Every atom in my body strained to jump into his lap and continue where we'd left off. I curled my nails into my palms until tiny bites of pain brought a little clarity.

"I'm afraid you'll have to resist."

To my surprise, he nodded. "Understood."

My jaw threatened to drop. I caught myself, then

shifted my gaze from his face. Now I'd successfully drawn the line, I didn't know what to do next.

He answered by stepping out and escorting me inside.

In my office, he calmly returned to the sofa. While I spent the next hour rewriting the same code.

I called it a night at six. He drove us home after stopping to pick up the takeout I'd ordered.

Over dinner, he asked me a bunch of work-related questions, probing my routines and those of my team. Any trace of the fever that overtook us in the restaurant and the parking lot was wiped from his features as he listened and made notes on his laptop.

Just before nine, he sat back in his chair, his eyes on his screen. "That's enough for today. I'll see what I can dig up with this info." His tone was impersonal as he stood and picked up the plates and empty cartons. He helped clean up and stack the dishwasher, maintaining a chilly distance that made my stomach muscles tighten.

You wanted this. Professional distance is good.

When we were done, I turned to leave.

"Remember, you need to let me know if you're going outside," he said.

My face felt stiff so I didn't even attempt a smile. "I haven't forgotten."

He stared at me for a beat then nodded.

In my den I made a stab at work for a solid hour before giving up and giving in to a burst of resentment. I swiveled in the seat and stared out the window.

Caleb probably thought he was only doing his job, but his interrogation had peeled back a thin layer of memories I wanted to keep buried.

Boston. My mother.

Frustration threatened to build as I paced from window to wall and back again. My restlessness eventually drove me to the cinema room and I halfheartedly settled for a new rom-com I wasn't really in the mood for.

I startled awake to a blank screen and a sore neck. When my disorientation cleared, I noticed a blanket that had been draped over me and there were cushions I'd dislodged in my sleep, which weren't there before.

My heart lurched as that warmth encroached again, teasing me with its comfort. I pushed it away, got up and stumbled upstairs to bed.

Caleb Steele, like everyone in my life, was a transient, *paid* presence.

Nothing else.

Sunday was a repeat of Saturday, minus the mind-melting making-out sessions, the probing questions into my sex life and the sexually loaded banter.

That set the course for the next three days.

On Thursday we returned to the Japanese restaurant and picked our way through an uncomfortable meal.

As he wove through light traffic on the way back to SDM, I glanced at him, that little morsel he'd let drop on Saturday returning like a nagging toothache.

Who was the client who'd triggered his rule? Was he or, as I suspected, *she*, still in his life?

At a stoplight he speared me with dark blue eyes. "Something on your mind?" His tone was cool. That plus the absence of his mocking eyebrow lift rattled me more than I cared for. It was like he had become a different person after the episode in the parking lot.

I reminded myself that I'd only known him for a handful of days.

That first night and day had been…out of the norm. Intense. We were both fighting for control. We'd reached an understanding and now he was focused on what he came here to do.

This was the real Caleb Steele. End of story.

So this unsettled sensation that had carved a small hollow in my stomach was misplaced. Right?

I looked away from his piercing eyes. "Nope. Nothing at all."

He drove on, dismissing me as coolly as he'd done for the past few days.

Unfortunately, the sensation knotted inside me wasn't as easy to dismiss. Admitting I wanted the dirty-tongued, brooding-eyed Caleb back was…hard.

I glanced out the window, frowning at my reflection when I caught myself biting my lip. I had more important things to dwell on than which version of my fixer I preferred. Besides, what the hell could I do? Crawl into his lap, drag my fingers through his hair and kiss him the way I'd wanted to do on Saturday before sanity returned?

The dragging sensation in my belly gave me the answer.

I avoided his gaze for the remainder of the journey.

The fretful but excited buzz in the air when we reached my floor was a great excuse not to hunt for an answer right then.

"What's going on?" Caleb asked as we entered my office.

"We're presenting a midseason upgrade on two SDM products to the board tomorrow. The day before is always a little frantic."

His gaze narrowed slightly as he watched me. "That doesn't include what you're working on, does it?"

"No. That's still confidential. But I'll be giving a presentation of my own to three of the board members tomorrow, too."

"Which members?"

"Chance and two of his colleagues." I couldn't keep the stiffness out of my voice.

He noticed. "He's coming here?" he rasped.

I swallowed at the volatile vibes oozing from him. "Yes."

His gaze narrowed on me for several heartbeats. "Okay, I'll need the names of the colleagues."

I gave him the names, unable to stop the chill spreading over my nape. "Why?"

His stare was direct. "Everyone who has access to you is a suspect until I catch this asshole. Don't underestimate anyone, Lily. And if you can help it, don't trust anyone, either. That way you'll avoid any nasty surprises."

He turned away but not before I caught a flash of pain in his eyes.

Add the confounding emotions coiling through me, it rooted me to the spot for several heartbeats until a knock on my door snapped me free. By the time I finished dealing with my team member's query, Caleb was on his phone.

We worked late into the night, then headed down to the seventh floor where the in-house catering staff had laid out a buffet-style meal in the dining room.

Although Caleb stayed close by, he didn't engage in conversation. I tried not to glance his way, but it proved almost impossible. Especially when Miranda slid into the seat next to him, and he gave her one of those smiles that had been absent for almost a week now.

I turned away, finished the chicken parmesan I didn't really want, while doing my best to reassure the two tech newbies on either side of me that they wouldn't tank their presentation tomorrow.

I wasn't sure what made me glance over at Caleb halfway through my conversation. His eyes were fixed on me, a ripple of muscle ticking in his jaw as he clenched his teeth.

Abruptly, he stood and walked around to where I sat. "Are you done eating?" He glanced pointedly at my plate.

"Yes."

"You ready to head out?" he asked, flicking a cold glance at one newbie, who cowered away from the arctic mountain glowering at him.

I considered calling Caleb out on his rudeness, but it had been a long, draining day. I really wanted to get out of here. And it had absolutely nothing to do with wanting to get him away from Miranda, who was eyeing Caleb with barely disguised hunger.

I swallowed a knot of irritation. "Don't stay too long, Miranda. I need you back here by seven."

Her gaze swung to me, and I swore I caught a flash of something nasty in her eyes. A moment later it was gone. "Sure thing, boss. I'll make sure you're all set to go."

Caleb's impatient hand gripped the back of my chair, and I rose.

Maybe it was the don't-mess-with-me vibes he gave off as we left the building, but nobody approached to talk to me. I continued with last minute prepping on my tablet right until we drove through the gates of my house. And then I couldn't hold back the grain of irritation that had grown since dinner.

I cleared my throat. "I need a favor," I said briskly.

He paused with a hand on the door. His eyebrow twitched but didn't exactly lift. "Normally, a request like that is couched in a more…friendly tone."

I fixed my gaze somewhere around his chest to avoid New Caleb's cool, disinterested expression. "Tomorrow is an important day for me. So I need you not to…" I paused, a little annoyed with myself for needing to utter the words.

"It would help if you actually complete the sentence?"

The mild mockery lacing the words made me forget not to look into his face. His eyes weren't disinterested. They were neutral. Enough to make that odd little band around my chest tighten.

To hell with this. "Stop flirting with my assistant," I snapped.

He sat back in his seat, his eyes narrowing. "Why?"

"Excuse me?"

"What do you care who I flirt with?" he drawled.

"You're supposed to be a professional. Do I really need to point this out to you?"

He gave a careless shrug.

"Fine. Your…attention hasn't impacted her work. *Yet*. But—"

"You're worried she's becoming preoccupied with getting into my pants and you have a problem with that?" The words were delivered with a little more of that zing I was used to.

Hot little fires began licking through my veins, sparking electricity that engulfed my breasts, stung between my legs. "I only have a problem with how it pertains to my work. She needs to be on her A-game for tomorrow. So, yes, I'd be grateful if you'd dial down the low-voiced charm, and all that *smiling*."

The smile I'd just denigrated lit up his face. It was slow and deadly. It was also so drop-dead magnificent that I couldn't look away. Couldn't breathe. Couldn't do anything other than absorb it. Bask in it and God help me, grow intensely, claws-out possessive over Caleb smiling at another woman like that. And right in that moment of admitting that I was mindlessly attracted to him, I wanted to die.

Especially when that smile turned stupidly smug.

"Why, Lily, if I didn't know any better, I would think you were jealous."

CHAPTER NINE

Caleb

I WATCHED HER stalk to the front door, her body stiff with outrage.

My smile dimmed as my gaze swept feverishly over her, greedily taking one of the few long glances I'd been reduced to stealing all week. A part of me remained pissed off that she'd put the brakes on what had seemed like a slam-dunk acceptance of the green light I gave her.

Hell, three insanely hot make-out sessions in twenty-four hours was a record, even for me, although that first time in the restaurant had been a simple exercise in taking her down a peg or two, but had quickly escalated into something mildly earthshaking.

Okay, nothing about what happened between us could be classified under *mild*. I would've fucked her in broad daylight in the front seat of my SUV if one of us hadn't come to our senses.

Still. The part I was having a hard time dealing with was how hard it'd been to stick to my own rules this week. I'd spent more than a few sleepless nights reliving

Lily's taste, enduring a raging—pun intended—storm in my cock I was yet to get under full control.

As I watched her stab the code to turn off the alarm, though, I couldn't help my gratification at this latest revelation.

"I'm not jealous," she denied hotly as if she'd read my thoughts.

I shut the front door and slid home the dead bolt. "Really? You're sure acting like it."

Her grip tightened on the satchel she never left home without. "Of course you would think that."

I strolled over to her. "I did wonder why you felt the need to instruct Miranda to come in on time tomorrow when she's never been late."

"And how would you know that?" she challenged huffily.

I cracked a little smile, watched her eyes drop to my mouth before she averted her gaze. The slow, torturous burn in my loins intensified. The wall I'd deliberately erected between us to help honor her wishes crumbled a little. I was tempted to give it a healthy kick, but deep down I knew she was right to want to keep things professional between us.

Besides, I wasn't sure I wanted to test my control just yet. Lily was as sensational as I imagined she would be. And that was with barely a taste.

"I know how to get the information I need," I answered her question.

Her eyes narrowed. "Was that what you were doing tonight? Gathering information?"

I shrugged. "Sometimes it's best to use honey, not vinegar."

She nodded and turned toward the stairs.

"Are you going to bed?"

Her eyes met mine for a second before she looked away, the pulse at her throat picking up speed. She let go of the satchel to drag her fingers through her hair. At some point this week, she'd repainted her short nails a dark purple shade that looked almost black. Something about the way it contrasted against her shock-white blond hair raised my temperature.

"No. I was thinking of going for a swim. I need the exercise to...de-stress a little."

Fuck, I had a dozen positions in mind to help her de-stress. And that was for starters. I forced the lid back on my runaway libido. "You nervous about tomorrow?" I asked.

She knew I was asking about Chance and tensed for a moment, and then she deliberately avoided the subject. "I shouldn't be. The code is working perfectly. But..." She shrugged.

I'd been looking into Chance Donovan and had a few thoughts on the bastard CEO. But I didn't want to add to her stress.

So, even though Lily in a sexy swimsuit and within touching distance was so not a good idea, I jerked my head toward the stairs anyway. "Go get changed. I'll meet you in the living room."

"Thanks," she said, looking relieved that I'd let the matter drop.

I stayed at the bottom of the stairs, unable to take my eyes off her perfect ass as she sprinted upstairs. Yeah, I was a glutton for punishment.

That punishment increased a hundredfold the moment she entered the living room. My hand froze on the French doors, and I swallowed hard.

She was wearing a see-through black mesh T-shirt over a burnt-orange bikini. Two things struck me hard just then. First, that while her signature black suited her alabaster complexion, the dark orange was even more flattering, drawing attention to her pint-size perfection.

Second, that the wall I'd built to contain my insane attraction and strict rules didn't stand a chance of staying up.

"Everything okay?" she asked, her eyes a little wide as she took in the joggers and T-shirt I'd changed into.

Fuck, no. "Sure." I held the door open for her.

She walked past me, trailing light, sensual perfume that made me want to bury my face in her neck. Her back view was just as spectacular as her front, the tight globes of her ass barely contained in the bikini bottom.

A dangerously high percentage of blood rushed south, emptying my head of every thought except the one that fixated on what I wanted to do to her body. "How long do you need?" I croaked, dropping onto the lounger and hitching up one leg before she turned and saw the steel rod tenting my pants.

She paused at the edge of the pool and glanced over her shoulder. The setting sun's rays worshipped her cheek, her arms, her stomach and thighs. "I normally swim a hundred laps. So…forty-five minutes?" she murmured.

"Yeah. Fine." *Wow, you'll be drooling like a brain-dead idiot next.*

She grabbed the bottom of her T-shirt and pulled it over her head. A groan rumbled up my throat as she dove cleanly into the water with the smoothness of a practiced athlete.

It took twenty laps for me to get myself back under

acceptable control. Of course she chose that moment to pause at the far end of the pool to smooth back her wet hair and slowly swivel her head until her gaze rested on me. Her lips parted as she sucked in air to regain her breath.

She didn't utter a word. Neither did I. And yet, a thousand conversations passed between us.

Later, I would appreciate that this was the moment we both accepted that we were far from done with each other. That the rules and barriers and words we'd thrown up in an attempt to stop this sexual juggernaut stood no chance.

She clung to the edge of the pool for a full minute, her sexy green eyes never wavering from mine. Then with a lithe twist of her body, she dove underwater.

Every cell in my body wanted to join her. If for nothing else, to cool down before the top of my head blew clean off. But I stayed put, counted down her laps until she reached ninety-eight.

I jumped up, grabbed a towel from the stack next to the lounger and was waiting when she climbed the shallow steps.

Just like last time, delicious droplets clung to her skin. I wanted to lick each and every one off, then concentrate on licking her between her legs.

Instead, I held out the towel. Her eyes met and clung to mine as she accepted it and wrapped it around her body. "Thanks."

My eyes drifted to the wet curl clinging to her cheek. Unable to resist, I smoothed it behind her ear, then went to retrieve her T-shirt.

"Let's get you inside." I didn't give one tiny shit that my voice was a gruff mess. Or that my cock still stood at attention. I saw her eyes drop to it before, reddening, she glanced away.

She followed me inside and lingered in the living room as I locked the doors. "Drink?" I needed one badly before I did something foolish.

She passed the towel through her hair before lowering it. "Umm… I shouldn't."

I handed back her T-shirt. "That doesn't sound like a definite no," I said, then held up my hands. "But I'm not trying to corrupt you or anything so if you want to head up to bed, don't let me stop you." The breath trapped in my lungs told a different story to the words falling from my mouth. I wanted her to stay. Badly.

She dropped the towel on the coffee table and shook her head. "No. I'll just lie in bed worrying about stuff. Or I'll be tempted to tinker with the code some more. Bad idea," she said with a laugh.

It was the first time I'd heard her laugh. The soft, tinkling sound hooked into me, feeding a need to hear more of it. "Okay, so what do you do to distract yourself?"

She looked away, fidgeted, then dragged the T-shirt over her head. "I normally read. Or watch a movie downstairs…"

It was an easy decision. "I vote for downstairs." She had a bar down there, after all. "I'll have a drink. You can join me. Or not." I cocked an eyebrow.

The barest hint of a smile curved her mouth as her gaze touched on my brow. "I get to pick the movie."

I shrugged. "Your theater, your choice. I'm just coming for the booze."

Her smile widened a little more.

We went down together, her bare feet slapping lightly on the polished wood. I crossed to the bar shelves stacked with expensive alcohol. She went to the sweets stand and returned with a large cone cup filled with assorted candy.

She popped a pink marshmallow into her mouth, then held out the cup to me. I chose a jellybean and pointed it at her. "These things will rot your teeth."

"Luckily I have an excellent dental plan." Her sexy grin exhibited perfect teeth.

I refocused on pouring my bourbon. "You sure you don't want anything?"

She inspected the row of drink bottles behind me. "Okay, I'll have a lemondrop martini, please."

I laughed. "You folded much easier than I thought you would."

She plucked another marshmallow from her supply before placing the cup on the counter. "I rarely fix it myself because it never comes out right. You look... comfortable behind the bar, like you know what you're doing."

Our eyes met. Locked. "So this is a test?"

Her lips slowly parted. "Maybe."

"And if I pass?"

Her gaze swept down for a moment before stunning green eyes met mine again. "I'll let you help me pick the movie."

I slowly set down the bourbon, biting my tongue against spilling what I really wanted for my prize. Hell, she knew it already. Knowledge flamed in her eyes. Whether she would choose tonight to do something about it was another matter.

I gathered the ingredients and watched her watch me fix her drink. I slid it across the counter to her, lifted my glass of bourbon and waited.

She picked up her glass, took a delicate sip. Her tongue slid across her bottom lip. My cock jumped. "It's good."

"Just good?"

Again, her eyes flicked to my raised eyebrow, and her mouth twitched. "Okay. It's perfect."

"You're welcome." I reached into the freezer, plucked out two ice cubes and dropped them into my drink. Anything to lower the inferno raging in my groin.

Grabbing her candy and drink, she hopped off the bar and headed for the red leather lounger with drink holders on either side.

Perfect for two.

On Saturday night, when another damned nightmare had ripped me from sleep, I'd wandered downstairs, heard the movie running and came to check on her. I'd toyed with waking her but with tensions running high, I thought it best to leave her alone. As I'd made her comfortable, she'd made a small, forlorn sound that ripped through me.

As I joined her now, questions crowded my mind. Asking more personal ones would mostly likely hurl us back onto the battleground. So I stuck to a less volatile one.

"I've ruled out most people on the list." Including her ex. A discreet probe into Scott Wyatt's activities showed he'd been mostly out of town in the weeks before the stalking started, and was currently engaged in a long-distance relationship with a new woman in Seattle. He was lucky he was out of my reach.

A trace of unease flitted over Lily's face. "Okay. So who's left?"

I paused. My answer could risk her acting differently

around the people left on the list. "I haven't been able to rule out Nordic Razor yet. Could he have seen what you were working on when you were online?"

She tucked her legs underneath her, rested sideways on the lounger, and took another sip of her drink. "No. I use a separate computer for social activities."

I set my glass in the holder. "Why Q?"

"What?"

"Cipher Q. What does the Q stand for?"

She toyed with a damp strand of hair. "What do you think it stands for?"

"I thought it was Quantum. But I'm going with Queen," I replied.

Her head dipped, that hint of shyness and innocence adding to her appeal. "It's silly, I know. And vain. But…"

"But you wanted to feel empowered at a time when things felt out of control?"

Her mouth dropped open a few seconds before she shut it. "I don't like it when you do that," she murmured.

"Do what?" I asked gently.

"See…too much."

"I won't hurt you, Lily. Not with any information you give me. I can promise you that."

After a moment, she nodded.

Grasping that tiny leeway, I probed softly, "How old were you when you started hacking?"

She looked a little trapped by my question, but she answered, "Thirteen."

"I'm guessing it was your stepfather who made you feel…less?"

A shadow crossed her face and she remained silent for a long time before she nodded. "He was saddled with me after my mom left. Every now and then he would let me feel his displeasure."

My fist tightened. "Did he hurt you?"

"Physically? No. In other ways…yes."

I took a sip of bourbon just for something to do so I didn't drive my fist through the wall behind me. "Tell me what he did."

Her nostrils quivered as she sucked in a breath. "I don't have all night."

"Then tell me exactly how you got involved with Chance."

"When I was fourteen, I hacked him. I was good back then, but I wasn't great. He hired another hacker to find me, and turned up at my house with the cops. He gave me a choice, work for him or go to jail."

"Your stepfather didn't tell him to get lost, I take it."

She gave a bitter laugh. "Not when Chance started throwing money his way, he didn't."

She flinched at my tight curse. I reached across the counter and placed my hand on hers. She stared at it with a sad smile before she inhaled long and deep.

"Anyway, between them they hammered out a deal that he'd pay my stepfather a monthly fee for my maintenance, then my college tuition fees on condition that when I left MIT I'd devote all my time to developing something big for him."

"The algorithm?" I asked, my chest and throat tight with the effort it took to keep my fury inside.

She nodded. "I had the beginnings of the idea back then."

"Why didn't you walk away when you turned eighteen or even twenty-one?"

Her lips tightened and she shrugged. "I gave him my word I wouldn't."

A simple answer, but such a powerful statement as to the true depths of Lily Gracen. I would've thought it impossible, but I grew even more attracted to her in that moment.

"And the Scott thing? How did you find out?"

She smiled unapologetically. "I hacked his phone records and confronted him."

"How did Chance take it?" I realized I was searching for another reason to punch the guy's lights out when I met him tomorrow.

"He claimed he was looking out for me. I called bullshit and threatened to walk then. He promised it would never happen again." The information was coming out in charged little bites.

"Lily—"

She shook her head. "No more. You're ruining the mood."

I cupped her cheek, my thumb caressing her lower lip until she had herself back under control. "Don't feel bad about letting me in. I know a little about how that feels like."

Wide green eyes locked on mine. "Really?"

I heard the throb of pain in my voice and inwardly grimaced. I could've answered differently, thrown her off with a shrug or said nothing at all. Instead, the last word I expected to say surged from my throat. "Yes."

She waited. Then a breath huffed out. "That's all you're going to give me?"

Curiosity swirled in her eyes, making my chest pound for a different reason. "Yes. I don't want to ruin the mood, either."

Her breath grew shaky. As did her hand when she raised her glass to take a healthy gulp. She stared at me for several heartbeats. Then, visibly shaking it off, she grabbed the remote and aimed it at the screen.

"Lowlights." Her command activated the lights, dimming the overhead lights and leaving only a set of lowlights running along the floor.

Onscreen, the system had grouped her entertainment into genres and then favorites. She clicked *favorites*. A long list rolled down the screen.

"These are all your favorites?" I asked skeptically.

"Uh-huh."

The title she clicked on caught my eye, and another raw memory spiked through me. *"The English Patient?"*

She glared at me. "It's a classic."

"If you want to weep into your martini glass the whole time then fall into a coma from boredom, sure."

"You've seen it?"

My teeth clenched as I toyed with evading. "Yeah, I've seen it. It was my mother's favorite, too."

Naked, hesitant curiosity lit her eyes. *"Was?"*

I threw back the remaining bourbon. What the hell… "She died. Fifteen years ago." Because she fell through the cracks. Over and over again until she hit rock bottom and never rose. I swallowed my bitterness as Lily leaned closer.

"When you were fourteen?"

I jerked out a nod. Silence throbbed between us, then I indicated the screen. "Are we gonna watch this movie or what?"

Her head swiveled to the screen, then back at me. She held out the remote. "The deal was you could help me pick. You've vetoed my first choice. Show me what you got."

I accepted it, allowing my fingers to graze hers. She exhaled sharply.

God, I wanted to feel that puff of breath on my face. Reluctantly, I turned to the screen. Surprisingly, only half of the movies were chick flicks. Top-notch detective movies and psychological thrillers had made the cut.

I frowned as the list kept going. "There are over a hundred here. How can they all be your favorite?"

She stared at me. "Is it too difficult? I can help you out if you want?" I caught a hint of teasing challenge.

I snorted and selected one.

She grimaced. "Uh, no. I love Bruce Lee but not tonight. The sound effects alone will give me a headache."

I scrolled some more until she laid her hand over mine. "This one," she breathed.

"Revenge?" It was the original movie with Anthony Quinn, Kevin Costner and Madeleine Stowe. I couldn't remember the plot line but I'd probably seen it. Movies had been a huge escape for Mom the few times depression released her from its merciless talons. To be honest, they'd been an escape for me, too, because for a blessed stretch of two or three hours, I could stop worrying about her. She'd even summoned a laugh when we watched a comedy.

"Yes. It doesn't have a high rating but I love it. Unless you want to find something else?"

I tore myself from the past. "This will do." I hit Play and pointed to her empty glass. "Do you want another?"

She stared wistfully at the martini glass. "No, I better not. I'll take a soda, though."

I grabbed a soda for her and bottled water for my-self. She broke the tab, curled her lip over the top and drank half the contents, while I forced myself not to stare at her throat.

The movie's plot became clear within twenty min-utes. Sex. Corruption. Forbidden lust. Betrayal.

I settled in and tried to give it my full attention. Lily set the cup of candy between us and stretched out her legs. She ate another marshmallow, then held out a jelly bean to me. I took it, chewed, and steeled myself not to stare at her exposed thighs. Or her flat belly beneath the mesh top. Or the slight mound of her pussy.

Jesus.

A few minutes later she shifted again, turning onto her side to face me as she slid one leg up against the other.

She rested her head on one arm, and started toying with the ends of her short hair.

Hell, something about the way she played with those white-blond tips turned me on beyond comprehension. A moment later her other hand dipped into the candy cup. She didn't pick one, just rummaged through it, her gaze still fixed on me.

"Are you going to settle down or are you planning on fidgeting through the movie?"

Dark-tipped fingers traced the edge of the cup.

"I still feel...wired," Lily stated, her voice hardly above a husky whisper.

Alcohol, sugar, unscripted revelations and lust didn't sit well together. Add the flimsy top and bikini she wore, and it was an explosion waiting to happen.

I grabbed the candy cup and moved it to the other

side of my seat. "Maybe you should stop stuffing your-self with sugar, then."

Her lower lip protruded in a sexy pout, drawing my eyes to the luscious curve.

Lily made a small, muffled sound under her breath. "Caleb."

God, *now* she chose to say my name voluntarily. In that damn dirty, cock-stroking voice.

Her free hand dropped onto the space between us, then drew tiny circles on the leather.

"Maybe it's time to call it a night." I didn't mean it. At all.

She dragged her lower lip between her teeth. "No. I…can't. I'm wound too tight," she whispered.

"Tell me what you need." *Hell of a time to be the better man, Steele.*

She blinked slowly, sultrily, and her hand bunched into a fist. A moment later her gaze swept over my chest, then dropped lower to caress my rigid cock. She took a deep breath. "I've decided to accept that pass."

I stopped breathing. "What?"

Beautifully lusty, gorgeously defiant eyes met mine. "You heard me. You gave me a loophole in your rule. I'm taking it."

Filthy little fires leaped through my body. "What exactly are we talking about?"

A wickedly saucy smile curved her lips. "You'll see. Wanna get my Bob?"

Shit. My cock was very ready and extremely capable. I gritted my teeth for a second. "Your little pink toy. You sure?" I rasped.

"I need release and the way I see it, I have two

choices. I can let you fuck me or help me some other way. I'm not ready for the first one yet."

What the hell did she have in mind? "Lily—"

"Are you in, Caleb?"

As if I could answer any other way. "Where is it?"

Hectic color stained her cheeks as she nodded to the small bathroom next to the bar. "Under the first blanket in the closet," she whispered.

I sucked in a sustaining breath and rose from the lounger.

Fuck, I pushed her into testing my self-control. Now my cock was hard enough to hammer nails, and my balls were on fire.

Way to go, champ!

I entered the bathroom and tossed the first blanket. The bright pink sex toy gleamed at me. I wanted to leave it there, tell her I didn't find it.

I could easily give her what she craved with my mouth. My fingers. My tongue. But I knew I wouldn't be able to stop there.

I grabbed the gadget and returned to find her half sitting up, her breathing elevated. That mesh top was driving me nuts. As for her bare, supple thighs and the shadowed space between them—

"We need some ground rules," she blurted. "We keep our clothes on, no matter what. Deal?"

Her eyes were wide and shiny, and goddamn it, she was the most beautiful I'd ever seen her. And I wanted to see her come so badly, my back teeth hurt from the need. "Deal," I croaked.

I crawled back onto the lounger and laid the vibrator between us.

She looked down at it, and fresh flames lit up her alabaster cheeks. "Caleb—"

"I'm yours to command, baby. Just tell me what you need."

"Kiss me," she instructed.

God, yes.

Spiking my fingers through her hair, I yanked her down and fused my mouth to hers, heard her sexy little whimper, right before she melted into me. I didn't need to cajole my way in. She opened her beautiful mouth and I licked my way inside, unable to stop from groaning as I got another taste of Lily.

She eased back against the seat. I followed until my chest was pressed against hers, her firm, plump breasts rubbing against me as she breathed.

I deepened the kiss, sliding my tongue against hers, biting the tip of it when I recalled how much she liked it last time. She rewarded me with a moan, the hands exploring my back quickening their caress. Her fingers traced the waistline of my joggers, then tentatively dropped to my ass. I bit gently on her top lip. Her nails dug into my ass, even as her legs parted to accommodate me.

The flames licking through my veins intensified as I broke away and glanced down between us. Less than six inches separated us. I only needed to drop down a fraction for my cock to brush her bikini-covered mound. And if I angled downward I would easily slide between her legs, rub the underside of my cock against her clit. Get her off that way.

My breath shuddered out as I glanced into her glazed eyes. At her bruised lips.

Fuck me.

She was in charge, and as much as it unsettled me, it was also the headiest thing I'd ever experienced.

Slamming on the brakes was hard. But I planted my hands on either side of her head, increased the gap between us and drew up my knees to bracket her thighs. From my position, I had an intoxicating view of her from head to toe.

"What now?" I rasped.

One hand scrambled blindly for the vibrator. Then hesitated.

"Go for it, sweetheart. Before my good intentions take a flying leap." Her breath kept hitching as if she couldn't catch it. When her gaze dropped to my mouth, I dropped my head and delivered a quick, hard kiss. "Now, Lily," I commanded hoarsely.

She brought it up between us, and flicked it on with her thumb. Noticing the low setting, I raised my eyebrow.

"I've never used number three before," she blurted.

I put my thumb over hers and flicked it up two more. "Then I'm glad I'm here for your first time." My grin felt as tight as the pressure in my groin as I returned to my original position. And waited.

Slowly, she lowered her hand, and then paused with the sex toy above her belly. Then she raised her gorgeous eyes to me. "You do it."

Fuck. I drew in a strangled breath. "You sure?"

She caught her lip between her teeth and nodded jerkily. She handed me the vibrator, then lowered her hand and drew aside the crotch of her bikini.

At the first sight of her pretty pink pussy, I nearly lost my mind.

Fighting the irrational jealousy rising within me, I

slid the vibrator against her wet clit. A sharp gasp broke from her lips as her back arched off the lounger.

My arms shook with the effort it took to stay upright. "Fuck."

"Oh…God." She shuddered as I pressed the vibrator harder against her clit. "Ahh…"

The scent of her wetness rose between us, triggering fresh agony in my balls. "God, your pussy smells incredible, Lily."

Another set of shudders unraveled through her, ending in her undulating her hips against the pink toy. Beneath the mesh and bikini top, her nipples were hard little points that begged to be tasted.

Saliva filled my mouth as I fought with the rampant urge to rip her clothes off and do just that. Instead, I contented myself with planting openmouthed kisses down her satin-smooth neck, licking the frantic pulse racing at her throat. Biting her earlobe.

"Caleb. Oh." The groan was dragged from her as her face pinched and her eyes rolled shut.

"Are you close, baby?"

She shuddered, her hips moving faster. "Yes… Yes!"

"Open your eyes. Look at me. I want to see your gorgeous eyes when you come," I instructed, barely recognizing my own voice.

Her lust-glazed eyes met mine. "Caleb… I'm coming," she said in a hushed whisper. "Oh!" Her hips exploded and she screamed.

My fists bunched hard, tension screaming up my spine as I locked my knees to stay put.

Dear God, she was glorious.

I lost the fight halfway through her release, and slanted my mouth over hers. Her lips clung to mine as

I devoured her every panted breath, desperate not to miss a moment of her glorious climax.

After an eternity, her convulsion died down. That was when I realized her arms and legs were locked around me. When the smell of her hit me, I knew I was in deeper trouble.

Clamping an arm around her waist, I lifted her off the lounger and staggered for the door.

"Caleb?" Her voice was still slurred.

"I'm taking you to bed," I said through clenched teeth.

Her breath hitched. "No."

"Don't worry. I'm not going to pressure you. You're going to bed alone. And we're definitely going to fuck," I promised, "but not until this shit is taken care of."

Her legs clamped tighter around me. Which delivered the fresh hell of having my eager cock sweetly cradled by her very wet pussy.

I stumbled on the stairs as she buried her face in my neck and gave a low moan. "But…what about you?" she whispered, performing a slow, torturous grind against me.

"I'll take care of it…later." My mouth drifted from the corner of hers to the delicate shell of her ear. "Or I'll save it for you."

She whimpered. A glorious sound. I tunneled my fingers in her hair and pulled her head back.

"Would you like that?"

Her blush deepened, but she met my gaze. "Yes."

I groaned, tightened my hold on her and vaulted up the stairs.

In her room, I pulled back the covers and set her down in the middle of the bed. Her legs stayed locked in place for a beat before she released me. I kissed her soft lips and reluctantly stepped back. "Get some sleep. I'll see you bright and early."

Resolutely, I headed for the door.

"Caleb?"

My hand tightened around the door handle, and I squeezed my eyes shut for a bracing second before I looked over my shoulder. "Yeah?"

She twisted a corner of the duvet between her fingers, making no move to cover herself. "Thank you. For…tonight."

My fevered gaze scoured her body to the shadows between her legs, unashamed of the savage hunger most likely blazing on my face. "Don't thank me just yet. I intend to fuck your lights out the second this shit is handled. And it won't be a nice, gentlemanly fucking. Good night, Lily."

CHAPTER TEN

Lily

MY INNER ALARM nudged me awake just shy of 5:00 a.m., after the soundest sleep I'd enjoyed since my stalker problem started. I stretched, rolled over and froze as memories of last night flooded in.

Heat surged through my body, pooling in my pelvis, before rushing up to engulf my face.

OMG!

I lay there, breath held, bracing myself for extreme vulnerability slash acute mortification. I'd bared parts of my past I'd never told another soul to Caleb. And then I'd let him use my vibrator on me!

Weirdly, neither sensation arrived. Emotionally, I felt unburdened, like a heavy cloak had been lifted off my shoulders. And neither by word nor deed had Caleb judged me.

Sexually, I felt…sensational. Like I'd won a grand prize in a contest I didn't even know I was competing in.

Great sex had always felt like a gift granted to other people, a sleight of hand everyone else had mastered but me. I wasn't ashamed to confess that was the reason why I invested in the very best sex toys. But…last night…

I came harder than I ever had…and we didn't even have sex. I was one hundred percent sure it had nothing to do with the higher setting on my vibrator. The only other time I'd tried the highest setting, all I could think about was the noise and what possible damage the overload of electricity was doing to my clit. It ruined the experience.

But last night I unlocked a previously unknown inhibiting door and been rewarded with an amazing experience.

The memory of him crouched over me, big, hot, wild, with barely restrained hunger stamped on his face, his hand between my legs, and dirty, beautiful words pouring out of his mouth…

Yeah, that certainly guaranteed the unforgettable encounter my instinct had been nudging me toward from the start.

I felt empowered, like I could do it all over again, no problem.

I gulped down the moan rising in my throat.

Despite laying down the caveat, there'd been a moment, right before that incredible climax hit me, when I'd wanted to beg Caleb to pull out his thick cock jutting boldly against his pants. Beg him to *fuck my lights out*.

His gruff, sexy promise echoed in my head, ripping free a ravenous moan. I wanted that. Badly.

Except it wouldn't happen until my stalker was caught.

My stalker.

My code.

The SDM presentation.

Reality drenched me like an icy waterfall, catapulting me out of bed and into the shower. Someone was still out there, watching, waiting for me to slip up. I clenched my teeth against the skin-crawling sensation that threatened to ruin my day and tried to regain my buzz.

I never quite got it back. My mood plummeted further when an email from Chance buzzed on my phone just as I was heading downstairs.

I entered the kitchen to find Caleb at the coffee machine. In the few seconds before he turned around, I hungrily ogled his V-shaped torso draped in a fitted navy blue shirt, tucked into tailored pants that framed his mouthwatering ass.

The ass I'd gripped all too briefly last night before he'd called a halt to my exploration.

He turned, two mugs of coffee in his hands. We both froze as his eyes met mine.

The memory of last night pulsed between us, hot and heavy. His heated gaze swept down and up my body, its intensity heightening with each pass. I was glad I'd taken extra care with my attire.

My black dress was a combination of a corset top and flared skirt, which I teamed with three-inch-heeled ankle boots. My makeup was flawless, too, with an added confidence-boosting layer of eyeliner and mascara, topped off with my favorite scarlet lipstick.

"Good morning," I murmured, eager for something to dissipate the charge rippling between us before I did something embarrassing, like stare at his crotch and wonder if he'd given in and jacked off last night or whether he'd kept to his promise to save it for me.

"Morning," he responded, striding forward to hand me the coffee.

We drifted to the center island, both lifting our mugs to take an idle sip while his eyes made another pass over my body. Then he reached out to touch the silver star dangling from the middle of my lace choker. "You look...incredibly beautiful," he said throatily.

My whole body reacted to his words, going from zero to furnace-hot in seconds. "Thank you."

His eyes slowly narrowed. "Something's wrong."

I waved my phone. "Email from Chance. He's bringing someone else to the meeting today."

He tensed. "Who?"

"He didn't say."

"Has he done that before?"

"Not at the last minute, no." I took another sip of coffee, swallowing it down with my anxiety.

"And you're worried," he observed.

I shrugged. "I can do without the extra pressure."

He set his mug down and cupped my cheeks. "I've watched you all week, batting away problems from your team without so much as pausing to look up from your keyboard. You'll kick ass today. I've no doubt."

Like last night, his gentle touch, together with the encouraging words, sent fierce prickles to my eyes. I blinked rapidly, dead certain I didn't want to cry in front of Caleb. "Thanks."

One thumb drifted along my jaw. "You're welcome," he murmured.

His gaze dropped to my mouth, and a different emotion swirled around us.

He stepped away first, picked up his cup and finished his coffee. "You ready to go?"

My nod was as shaky as the emotions zipping through me.

In the hallway, he picked up the waist-length jacket I dropped next to my satchel and held it out for me. I stood in front of him, put my arms through the sleeves, secretly breathing in the heady scent of aftershave and pure man. When I went to do up the single button, he brushed my hands away, pulled the lapels close and secured it.

Then he gripped my waist tight and pulled me back into his body. "I don't know how well you slept last night," he breathed in my ear, "but mine was pretty damned fucked because all I could think about was how magnificent you looked when you came. Just thought you should know."

I was struggling to breathe as he shrugged into his leather jacket and we left home without exchanging another word.

What could I say? That knowing he hadn't slept made my panties wet? To hell with waiting for my stalker to be caught. I wanted him to pull over and bang me on the backseat.

Conversation became redundant as his phone blared to life. He reached for it, his brows creasing when he looked down at the screen.

"Ross," he answered with a cool voice. "Yes, Maggie told me you've been trying to reach me. I've been a little busy." His eyes flicked to me before returning to the road. "What can I do for you?"

Traffic was light, and with the radio in the SUV set to low, I heard the other voice on the line. "The band won't take me back."

Caleb suppressed a sigh. "Have you been showing up for rehearsals like we agreed?"

"Every day. I even blew off my weekend plans to put in some extra work. They said it was too little, too late."

"It's only been a week. Maybe they're testing you to see whether you'll disappoint them again. Where are you right now?" Caleb asked.

There was a moment's hesitation before Ross-who-ever-he-was answered, "At the Beverly Hilton."

A muscle rippled in Caleb's jaw. "Didn't we agree you wouldn't go back there again?"

"Yeah, but if the guys won't take me back then what's—?"

"You better not be thinking of pulling that stunt again or I'll hang up right now and block your number permanently," Caleb interrupted harshly.

"I won't… But it's hard, man," the other man whined.

"That's what happens when you let people down, Ross. They stop trusting you." His voice gentled. "If you really want this, you just have to keep trying. They'll come around eventually."

"And if they don't?"

"Then you have to find answers elsewhere. You're talented. You just need to take a little more responsibility for your life. Ultimately, it's down to you whether you want to succeed or fail."

"I…want this. The band," Ross said.

"Then you know what you have to do."

A sigh echoed down the line. "Yeah. Umm…thanks, man."

"You can thank me by checking out of that hotel and getting your ass back home." He hung up and slid his phone back into his pocket.

Silence throbbed through the vehicle for a few blocks.

"You're good at this… Being a fixer."

The corners of his mouth lifted, but the smile didn't quite reach his eyes. "Thanks. That's high praise coming from you."

"I mean it. It can't be easy dealing with people who aren't always receptive."

He eyed me. "Are you including yourself in that?"

I hid a grimace. "Maybe. But what you said to him, just now...is that why you're a fixer? Because people let you down?"

His face tightened. "That's too heavy a conversation for this time of the morning, sweetheart."

"You're avoiding."

"And you're searching for something to take your mind off your meeting. This subject isn't it, Lily." There was a touch of warning in his voice.

"Why not? I've told you my secrets. You owe me something. *Quid pro quo*. Isn't that what it's called?"

His lips flattened. But he blew out a breath a moment later. "Yeah, a bunch of people let me down. But more than that, they let my *mother* down when she needed them the most. It's not a good feeling, being that helpless, so fixing became my thing."

"When did you start?"

"Officially? When I was twenty. Unofficially, shortly after my mother died. There was a lot of fixing to be done in Trenton Gardens." There was a hard, bitter note in his voice that drew shivers down my arms.

"I don't know where that is."

"Consider that a good thing, baby."

I looked at his rigid profile, and burning with a need I couldn't suppress, I tapped the name into my phone.

And grew colder. "Trenton Gardens, home of the most notorious gangs in South Central LA. Five people are killed there *every week*!" I read out loud with growing horror.

A flash of anger lit his eyes as he glanced at the phone, but then he gave a grim shrug. "Not exactly fairy-tale reading, is it?"

I put my phone away, my chest tightening with sympathy for this man with the hard exterior and flashes of tenderness. I wanted to know more, uncover his layers.

"I hear you sometimes," I murmured.

His body tensed. "Excuse me?"

"In the night. You don't sleep very well, do you?" I probed gently.

"What makes you think I'm not checking on things? Keeping you safe?"

"Are you?"

His fingers tightened around the steering wheel. "Leave it alone, Lily."

"My mother left just before I turned eight. I didn't sleep through the night for a year," I blurted. "My stepdad and I woke up one morning and she was…gone. Left a note to say she was never coming back and we shouldn't try to find her. Even after we received papers the next week from her lawyer granting my stepfather full custody of me I still thought she would come back. Stephen was sterile and couldn't have children of his own. That's the only reason he kept me."

Caleb cursed under his breath. "That's his loss, Lily, not yours."

I attempted to shrug his sympathy away, but my shoulders didn't comply. "I wasn't entirely blameless. It…hurt, knowing my mother could leave without a second thought, and my stepfather would've walked away if he had children of his own. I acted out. Sometimes."

"That's still not an excuse for what he did."

"I know, but…" I shrugged.

"Deep down you wish things had turned out differently," he said.

I sniffed away the unexpected tears. "Stupid, right?"

"No. Not stupid at all," he murmured, reaching out to glide a finger down my cheek.

Damn, there he went, being all gentle again. A fat drop rolled down my cheek.

He cursed again as he turned off the ignition. A distracted look outside showed we were in SDM's parking lot. It was still early enough that there were only a handful of cars around, the nearest one six bays away.

When his thumb brushed my chin, I tried to pull away, more than a little terrified of the softening happening inside me. He clamped his fingers in my hair, forcing me to look at him.

One brow was cocked, but his eyes were gentle. "I told you this was too heavy for this time of the morning. You should listen to me more often."

Another tear slipped free. I tried to laugh it away. "I have no idea why I'm crying. I'm over all of that. Counting the days until I put him and Chance in my rearview."

His fingers tightened on my nape. His other hand patted his lap. "Come here," he commanded.

My breath caught. "Why?"

"So I can make you feel better," he answered, his voice lower, deeper, curling around my turbulent emotions.

I shouldn't.

I really, *really*, shouldn't.

My hands slowly went to my seat belt, freeing it despite the voice screeching warning at the back of my head. Caleb's seat, already extended fully to accommodate his long legs, afforded me plenty of space as I crawled into his lap.

The hand on my nape speared into my hair and the other clamped one hip.

"Open your jacket," he instructed.

Hands shaking, I complied.

The sun wasn't fully up yet and the tinted windows shielded us as I braced my knees on either side of him. The moment my hands landed on his shoulders, he pulled me down and fused his lips to mine.

Caleb ravaged my mouth like I was his last meal, and I was more than happy to be devoured.

Between my legs, his erection thickened, pressing insistently against me. Shamelessly turned on, I ground against him, earning his tortured groan. We kissed until the need for more oxygen forced us apart. He kneaded my ass, encouraging me to grind against him. The feeling was intensely exquisite.

God, I could come from just rubbing my clit on his cock.

The thought drew a hungry moan but when I tried to dive back into the kiss, he stopped me.

"I didn't see a zipper on your dress when I helped you with your jacket earlier. Where is it?" he demanded hoarsely.

I motioned dazedly to my left rib cage.

"Take it down for me, baby," he said, his eyes still consuming me.

My racing heart tripled its tempo but I couldn't have stopped myself if a freight train was bearing down on me. I lowered the zipper until the corset gaped to reveal my breasts.

Caleb stared at me for another tense second before his gaze dropped. He exhaled sharply. "Fuck." His hand dropped to brush the back of his knuckles over one tight nipple, making me jerk against him. "I wondered whether these would be pale or dark." His gaze flicked to my face, absorbing my reaction as he repeated the gesture over the twin peak. "I have no clue which I would've preferred because seeing them now…they're fucking perfect." The words ended in a groan as he yanked me forward and clamped his mouth around one tight bud.

"Oh, God!"

He suckled me, hot and urgent, then flicked his tongue mercilessly over the sensitive bud, all the while dragging my damp center back and forth over his erection.

He transferred his attention to the other nipple, catching the freed, wet bud between his thumb and finger.

Stars exploded across my vision. "Yes!"

My fingers dug into his hair, desperate to keep him right where he was. I threw my head back as my hips took on a life of their own, fixated on riding him to the bliss that hovered on the horizon.

"Holy fuck, you're beautiful," he groaned against me, staring up at me with an intensity I couldn't fathom.

"Caleb…"

"You have no idea how gorgeous you are, do you?"

I couldn't breathe. This man was unraveling me, piece by piece. Body and soul. And I couldn't think of a single reason to stop him.

My body was a knot of seething sensation, waiting for some unknown directive to explode. Caleb wrapped one hand around my throat, restricting but not hurting. The other slipped beneath my dress and nudged my panties aside.

My fingers dug into his shoulders.

"I wasn't going to. But I need to feel you, Lily."

"Yes." Agreement was as easy as breathing, my need unstoppable.

His eyes hooked into mine, Caleb dragged his tongue across my nipple as he sank one thick finger inside me.

A tight scream erupted from my throat. He added a second finger and pleasure rained on me, quickening the movements of my hips as I chased ecstasy.

"Damn, you're so fucking tight," he exclaimed harshly, his breathing a ragged mess. "I can't wait to bury my cock inside you."

"Caleb…" I couldn't form any other words other than his name as he drove me insane with his fingers.

Sweet vortex swirled closer, sucking me down.

The hand around my throat bore me down onto piston-fast fingers. His thumb circled my clit and pleasure like I've never known before completely unraveled me. I came hard.

Somewhere in the midst of blinding ecstasy, Caleb covered my mouth with his, riding the waves with me until my convulsions ebbed away.

I collapsed in a boneless heap on top of him, panting like a bitch straight out of heat. He rained kisses on my neck and jaw, his hand caressing my ass.

"You okay?" he asked gruffly in my ear.

I hummed, mindlessly floating on a sea of bliss. The fingers inside me crooked, making me gasp one last time before he pulled out.

He gently nudged me upright, made me watch as he put his fingers in his mouth and licked off my essence. A fierce blush lit up my skin as he pressed his mouth against mine. "You taste even more sublime than I thought you would. The list of what I'm going to do to you is growing by the hour, baby. I've just added eating your pussy for hours to it."

I groaned, my senses firing up all over again. Before my orgasm-addled brain could return to reality, I scooted sideways and reached for his belt.

He tensed. "Lily?"

Maybe it was the orgasms that made me bold. Maybe it was his words of praise that tapped into a reserve of strength inside me. Either way, I slowly brushed my fingers over his mouth before replacing them with my own. "Shh," I whispered. "You're not the only one who gets to bestow awesome gifts this morning. I'm feeling generous, too."

His eyes widened a touch, right before his gaze dropped to my mouth. And locked, with blazing hunger flaring in his eyes. "Lily..." Hoarse anticipation thickened his voice.

"Will you let me, Caleb?" I lowered his zipper and slipped my hand beneath the waistband of his boxers. "Make us both feel good?"

He slammed his head against the headrest and groaned, long and hard and pained. "Do you really expect me to refuse an offer like that?"

I pulled him out, gasped and just...stared. *God.* He was huge. Thick and hard and insanely hot. Caleb's cock was everything I'd dreamed it would be and more. "You're beautiful." Tentatively, I stroked his hard length.

A rough sound erupted from his throat. "Dammit, Lily…"

Trepidation threatened to overcome me as the difference between watching a few porn clips and giving my first blowjob hit home.

I stroked him harder, loving the velvet-steel feel of him, loving the way his teeth gritted and his cheekbones flushed with color.

Lost in my ministrations, I startled when he cursed, "Fuck, stop licking your lips like that and put your gorgeous mouth on me before I come."

Heart racing, I slowly lowered my head and kissed his crown. A hiss flew from his lips as his hand slid up my back. I trailed kisses over his length, and then dragged my tongue up the underside of his cock, earning myself another deep groan.

Still sliding my hand up and down his glorious shaft, I flicked my tongue in rapid succession over his slit. His hips jerked against my mouth and frantic fingers dug into my hair. "Fuck!"

I sucked and pumped him with long, even strokes, establishing a rhythm that drew harsh pants from him.

"Yes! Fuck, yes, just like that," he croaked, his other hand fumbling for my breast.

Sensation curled through me as he fondled me almost frantically, his movements growing jerkier as I kept up a relentless pace on his cock.

A glance up showed his eyes squeezed shut, his chest heaving as he sucked in desperate breaths.

I reached between his legs, stroked his balls, and his fingers tightened painfully in my hair.

"God, Lily, don't stop. Don't fucking stop."

Impossibly, he thickened in my mouth. I drew him deep, right to the back of my throat and held still, glorying in his utter lack of control when he ground himself mercilessly against me.

"Take it. Fuck, take it all," he panted, right before a pure, animalist growl rumbled from his chest, then erupted in a hoarse shout as he came furiously in my mouth.

I swallowed him down, the salty muskiness of him weirdly addictive. When his body sagged against the seat, I licked him clean, then allowed him to pull me upright.

"Jesus, Lily. That was sensational," he breathed against my mouth.

The smile that curved my lips was pure feminine power. My first blow and I hadn't sucked at it. A wicked little laugh broke loose before I could stop it.

"Enjoying your power, are you?" he croaked.

"Maybe," I replied breathlessly.

He pulled me in for a deep, long kiss. When we parted, we stared at each other for several heartbeats, both adjusting to the shifting landscape beneath our feet.

His gaze scoured my face; then his thumb brushed my lower lip.

After he zipped himself up, he reached into the center console and handed me packet of tissues. I took one and reached between my legs.

He caught my wrist. "No. Not there. I want you to walk around the office today with a reminder of how good this moment felt. Each time you get anxious, re-

member this moment. Remember that you're phenomenal. Okay?"

The huge lump that rose in my throat prevented me
from speaking. After I nodded, he took the tissue from
me, and gently wiped my smeared lipstick. Then he
wiped his own mouth before reaching for my satchel
and the small makeup bag I kept in there.

He watched as I repaired my makeup, his intense
gaze fixed on my face. Only then did he zip me back
up, button my jacket and let me slide back into my seat.

"You ready?"

I took a deep breath and let my gratitude show in
my smile. "Yes."

His return smile was gentle if a little dazed around
the edges. "Let's go."

The morning presentation went without a hitch,
with an eager audience comprising the tech media
and bloggers, applauding when the two-hour event
was done.

Over the years, Chance and I had perfected the art
of being in the same room but speaking only the barest
minimum to one another.

Afterward, I returned to my office with Chance.
Caleb had grudgingly agreed to keep out of sight while
I dealt with Chance but I knew he was nearby, and that
gave me a layer of comfort I didn't know I needed till
it was time for the second presentation.

The beta test started off well, my tweaks making the
algorithm as fast as I promised it would be.

Right up until the moment the compression sequence
slowed to a crawl. My heart jumped into my throat.

Seventeen excruciating seconds ticked by before it sped up again.

But the blip was the only thing that mattered when the screen turned black and the lights went back up in the conference room.

CHAPTER ELEVEN

Lily

"I CAN FIX IT," I blurted. "It's just a small area of the code."

Chance looked furious. "We thought these wrinkles would've been ironed out by now."

"I still have three weeks of beta testing before the final deadline."

Walter Green, the man Chance had brought with him, frowned. "You said it would be ready, Donovan."

"I was assured it would be," Chance responded.

I ignored the men and fired up my laptop. Scrolling through the code, I zeroed in on where the problem was. Heart pumping, I forced myself to analyze it line by line. After forty lines, I stopped. "It's fixable," I repeated. "But I'll need time."

"How much time?" Chance snapped.

I bit my lip. "A week. Ten days, tops."

Silence greeted me.

Walter Green rose and left the room without saying a word. The other SDM executives also left.

Chance Donovan's gray eyes lanced me. The rest of him looked as harmless as a middle-aged CEO with a wife and three kids could look. But from the moment we met, I'd glimpsed a layer of menace in his eyes that pushed all my self-preservation buttons. "This is disappointing, Lily," he rasped.

I forced myself not to waver. "Who's Walter Green?"

"He's the guy who decides whether SDM sinks or swims. Delivering this algorithm, correctly and on time, and earning the freedom you claim to so badly crave, feeds directly into that. Is that clear enough?" he said.

"Yes," I murmured.

"Good. Now, what's this I hear about a new consultant?" he asked.

I struggled not to tense up as I trotted out the line Caleb and I practiced. "He's from LA. He's helping me with preliminary info on a possible gaming app my team is working on."

Suspicion flickered through his eyes. "Why don't I know about this? And why is he staying at your house?"

Why wasn't I surprised he knew Caleb was staying with me? "Because this is still *preliminary.* And because I don't need your permission to have a houseguest."

His eyes narrowed and he didn't speak for a long time. "Remember what's riding on this project, Lily," he warned, then left without further comment.

I buried my face in my hands.

A minute later Caleb arrived, swiveling my chair to face him before tugging my hands down. He'd been listening on my laptop so I didn't need to repeat what had happened. His solid presence took away some of my apprehension.

"Apart from my regret that I wasn't here to punch

that asshole in the face, the problem is only a minor bump in the road, right?"

"Maybe. Maybe not."

He frowned, crouching down in front of me. "Meaning?"

"The mistake looks…sophisticated. I triple-checked everything yesterday. I could've missed it—"

"You think you were hacked?" he asked.

The icy hand on my nape wouldn't let go. "I don't think so but it's possible…" I stopped as another thought occurred to me.

"What?"

"I added a last-minute tweaked version this morning from the team."

"Which team?"

"Sanjeet's team. But—"

His fingers brushed my lips, halting my words. "You want to think the best of everyone. I don't want to take that away from you, but you have to accept sooner or later than not everyone is decent."

My heart lurched. "I know, but I trust them."

"Give them the benefit of the doubt if you want. Let me worry about who's at fault here. Okay?"

Chest tight, my gaze settled on my laptop. "What's their end goal, Caleb?"

"The stalking is most likely to keep you off balance while they try to get their hands on what you're working on."

The thought drew a horrified shudder. "That can't happen."

"It won't," he ground out. With a decisive click, he shut the lid. "It's almost eight. You've been up since five this morning. I'm taking you home."

I shook my head. "I can't. The team always goes out to celebrate after a presentation. They'll expect me to be there."

"Where's it happening?"

"Q Base in Cupertino."

He pulled out his phone to relay the instruction to his security team. Then he cupped my shoulders. "You're officially clocked off for the day. Understood?"

Feeling numb, I nodded.

I was grateful when Maggie called and kept Caleb on the phone for most of the time it took to drive to Q Base.

Thumping music when we entered the club further prevented me from making meaningful conversation with Caleb or my team.

I exchanged high fives with anyone who stopped at the VIP lounge reserved for SDM, but the first chance I got, I headed to the main bar.

"You want a lemondrop?" Caleb leaned down to ask in my ear.

Memories of last night flooded in, knocking aside a bit of my melancholy. "Not unless you're making it," I said before I fully grasped how revealing my answer was. His lips curved in a smug smile. "They don't make it that well here. I'll have a noche azul," I added in a rush.

He ordered my drink and bourbon for himself.

Since it was early by clubbing standards, we had most of the dance floor to ourselves. But an hour later the place was packed.

I excused myself to go to the ladies' room, and returned to find Miranda seated next to Caleb. Frozen, I watched her lean in close and whisper in his ear.

A smile crept up his face but he shook his head. She leaned in closer, her bare leg sliding against his.

Hot, green bile curdled in my gut, merrily aided by the two cocktails I'd consumed. I wanted to stalk over, uproot her by the hair and lay my claim on him.

But other than the two orgasms he'd given me, a few shared confidences and a promise to screw each other's brains out sometime in the future, what hold did we have on one another? For all I knew, Caleb could be gone from my life this time next week.

The thought slashed through me, sharp and unexpectedly agonizing.

I made a U-turn, heading for the bar. Someone stepped in front of me. He looked familiar.

Mark, the ex who'd turned out to be harmless.

"I thought that was you," he said.

"Hi." I summoned a bright smile.

"Long time, no see."

"Yeah…"

He cocked his head at the dance floor. "Wanna dance?"

I looked over my shoulder. Caleb's eyes were fixed on me, narrowing as it flicked between Mark and me. Even from across the wide space, I witnessed tension climbing into his body.

I turned back around. "Sure, why not?"

Mark grinned. We headed to the dance floor and, with a sense of wild abandon, I threw myself into the dance. Seconds later Caleb materialized beside me.

"You. Beat it," Caleb snarled at Mark.

Like a true analyst, Mark assessed the situation, saw he was on a losing streak and beat a hasty retreat.

Furious blue eyes glared at me. "What the fuck are you doing?"

I lifted an eyebrow. "I should ask you the same thing. You just deprived me of my dance partner."

"You said you were going to the bathroom," he accused.

"I did. Only when I returned, you seemed…busy."

His jaw clenched. "So you decided to let some punk drool all over you?" he bit out.

I shrugged and his gaze dropped to my cleavage. I discarded my jacket a while ago, and without it my attire had transformed from quirky but acceptably professional to risqué.

"Not just some guy. I let my ex *dance* with me. Now that you've driven him away, are you going to take his place or just growl at me? You're certainly putting on a great show for our audience."

He didn't so much as flick a glance at said audience. He stepped closer, towering over me. I tilted my head, met his furious gaze full-on. Then I placed my hands on his waist. He tensed. Still watching him, I began to move, swaying my hips to the slower tempo of the song now playing. Then I added subtle shoulder shimmies.

His gaze dropped again to my cleavage and a light shiver rolled through him. I dragged my nails across his abs as I swayed deeper. His hand landed on my back and yanked me closer.

"Are you trying to make me lose my shit, Lily?" he rasped in my ear.

I pouted. "I'm just trying to *dance*."

He stared down at me for tense seconds. "Fine. Let's dance."

Over the next five songs, Caleb effortlessly proved

how incredible he was on the dance floor. Smooth moves drew increasing attention until every pair of female eyes was fixed on him.

His wicked smile flashed with increasing frequency, until I was turned on beyond belief.

Enough to make me forget my disgruntlement. Enough to make me grip his hand tight as he led me off the dance floor.

"Want another drink?" he asked as we found a quiet spot near the bar.

"No, thanks."

"Okay." He smoothed a lock of hair behind my ear, then caressed my jaw.

I looked into his gorgeous face and smoldering eyes.

Heart hammering, I bit the inside of my cheek. It was now or never. "Caleb?"

"Yeah?" His voice was gruff, as if the feelings swirling inside me gripped him, too.

"I don't want to wait."

He pulled back, blue eyes piercing as they searched mine. "If this is because of what happened at your presentation—"

"No, it's not." I swirled my tongue over my lip, nerves consuming me. "Please, Caleb. You said you wouldn't hurt me with anything that happens while on this case. I'm saying the same to you. I want you..."

Then he leaned in, one hand braced on the wall above my head. "Just so we're clear, you want me to what, exactly?" he demanded.

I slid my hand up his chest, over his shoulder to his nape and drew him down to me. "I want you to break your rule and take me home," I whispered in his ear. "I want you to take my panties off. I want you to undress me. Or I… I can keep my dress on if you want. And I want you to fuck my lights out. Like you promised."

A deep shudder rolled through him. He continued to stare at me for several heartbeats. "Jesus." He buried his face in my neck, breathed out harshly, then plucked my hand from around his neck. "I knew I wouldn't be able to hold out for much longer. Are you sure?"

"Yes."

His jaw clenched as he tried to fight it for one more minute. Then: "Let's go."

Each mile from Cupertino back home felt like an eternity.

I was hot, getting hotter and wetter every time I glanced at Caleb's tense profile. At the thick rod of his cock pressing against his fly. He changed lanes suddenly, his thighs flexing as he stepped on the gas.

"I like the way you drive."

He flicked me a heated glance. "I like the way you're looking at me."

On impulse, I reclined my seat by thirty degrees and propped up my legs on the dashboard. The skirt of my dress slid down to midthigh.

Heat turned to flames. "Christ, Lily, you're going to get me arrested. I swear to God, if I get pulled over before I've fucked your phenomenal pussy, I'll spank your sweet ass until you can't sit down for a week."

Why did the thought of that sound insanely heavenly? "I have bail money. I'll help you out," I said, sliding my skirt higher.

He swerved into the faster lane, splitting his fevered attention between the road and my thighs. Then he groaned. "Stop. Please, baby, let me get us home in one piece. Then you can show me this insanely sexy, naughty side of you."

My fists bunched. "I don't know if I can wait."

"Well, I'm not fucking you on the side of the road our first time, that's for damn sure," he growled. He reached over and gripped my thigh, pressing my flesh a little roughly before snatching his hand away. "Behave." His terse plea almost made me smile.

"Okay." I released my skirt and draped my arms around the headrest, exposing a generous amount of breasts.

"For fuck's sake! You think that's better?" he rasped hoarsely.

"Hmm. Maybe I'll take a nap. Wake me up when we get home?"

He cursed again as I closed my eyes. A few sharp turns threatened to dislodge my feet from the dashboard. My saucy smile melted away as the minutes ticked by. By the time we arrived home, I was as breathless and as on edge as Caleb.

He turned off the ignition without glancing my way. Stepping out, he stalked over to my side and yanked the door open. His chest rose and fell rapidly as he scoured my reclined body.

Slowly, his eyes locked on mine, he reached over and unsnapped my seat belt. When I attempted to rise, he pressed a hand against my midriff. With his other hand, he trailed his fingers down my inner thigh. Torturously, he slipped beneath my skirt, just as he did this morning. When he reached his destination, his fingers fingers boldly against my mound, cupping me through my panties.

"Jesus, Lily, you're fucking soaked," he muttered with a groan.

He circled his fingers, applying pressure over my engorged clit. I whimpered before I could stop myself.

The sound triggered him into action. He scooped me up, kicked the door shut and strode to the front door. Opening it, he set me down and deactivated the alarm. "Stay put."

The security check took less than five minutes. Anticipation had me breathless by the time he trotted back downstairs. On the second to last step he stopped, hands clasped behind his back.

"Come here." The order was gravel-rough.

On shaky legs, I teetered over to him. With his elevated position, my eyes were level with his fly. And excruciatingly aware of what lay behind it.

He stared at me. Then he nodded at his crotch. "See what you've done to me?"

My head bobbed up and down.

"What are you going to do about it?" he demanded thickly.

I swallowed as a dozen erotic images flashed through my mind, all starting and ending with my hands on his body. My hands found his chest, felt the hard muscles shift beneath my touch, then trailed over his abs to his waist.

Then, breath held, I slowly slid his belt free. Twisted open his button and lowered his zipper.

His broad chest expanded in a deep intake of breath, his eyes dark pools of hunger tracking my every move. Whether it was those incisive eyes or my own insecurities that suddenly pummeled me, I wasn't sure. I froze, my mouth drying as I struggled to breathe.

* * *

With a snatched breath, I slipped my hand beneath his waistband and closed my fingers around him.

His breath hissed out between gritted teeth. He swallowed hard but didn't move an inch. I tugged his pants and briefs lower, exposing the cock that had fueled more lurid fantasies all day.

I stroked him once. Twice. He grew thicker, his dick pulsing in my hold. Emboldened, I tightened my grip, pumped him a few more times.

A tortured groan rumbled from his throat as his fingers sank into my hair. "Fuck, Lily, that feels so good."

I stepped closer, breathed in his earthy scent. But it wasn't enough. I wanted more. I wanted to devour him. I yanked down his pants, cupped his heavy balls. He groaned again, a drop of precum glistening at his broad head.

I flicked my tongue against his slit and he jerked against me. I went to taste him again, but his fingers clenched in my hair, pulling me away.

"No." The denial was torn reluctantly from his throat.

My fingers tightened around him, making his abs clench hard. "Caleb, I... I want you in my mouth." This morning hadn't been enough. I wanted more.

He shuddered, but still shook his head. "I'd love for you to blow me again, sweetheart, but right now, I'm dying to be inside you."

Before I could protest, he scooped me up again like I weighed nothing, pivoted and hauled ass up the stairs. The hallway passed in a blur, the door to my bedroom slamming shut to his kick.

He set me down on the side of the bed. Eyes pinned to mine, he made short work of his buttons and shrugged off his shirt. He was ripped and tanned all over, hairless except for the thin strip of silky hair that arrowed from his belly button to frame his groin.

"You're so hot," I gushed, unable to stop myself.

Dark color flared across his cheekbones, and his nostrils flared as he toed off his shoes and socks. "Keep talking like that and you won't get to walk straight for a week," he growled.

The very idea made me weak. I sagged onto the bed with a pathetic whimper.

With a smug smile, Caleb bent over me, pressed his forehead against mine as he nudged me backward onto my elbows. He grabbed my knees and made room for himself between my thighs, then fused his lips with mine.

The kiss was ravenous to the point of decimation. Strong fingers kneaded my calves, then drifted down to tug off my shoes. He continued kissing me as his hands reversed direction, trailed up my thighs to slip beneath my dress. He started to pull down my panties, then halfway through he muttered under his breath and ripped it free.

At my gasp, he smiled against my lips. "Sorry."

"You're not really, are you?" I challenged between kisses.

"No," he confirmed, then sucked my tongue into his mouth in a move that melted my brain.

God, the man could kiss. I'd lost the ability to think straight when he pulled away. From his back pocket he took out a pack of condoms and tossed it on the bed.

I was staring at the box, wondering if I would be lucky enough to get through the pack by morning, when he grabbed my thighs and dropped onto his knees. Utterly captivated, I watched Caleb trail his tongue slowly up one inner thigh, then the other, but maddeningly staying away from my needy center.

"Get the lights up in here. I want to see your beautiful pussy properly," he said as he bit lightly on my flesh.

Pleasure shivering through me, it took a moment to realize the only light in the room was the one on my dresser, set to come on automatically at nightfall.

My breath puffed out as my lungs remembered how to work. "Lights," I croaked. Nothing happened. I cleared my throat. "Lights."

The lamps on my nightstand flared softly, chasing away the shadows. Baring me to Caleb's avid gaze. His mouth dropped open, a hot breath escaping as he stared.

And stared.

I squirmed. "Caleb…"

"Shh. Give me a moment," he rasped.

A moment to what? I squirmed harder.

He lifted his gaze and his eyes were on fire. "You're fucking exquisite, Lily." Hunger and worship throbbed in his voice.

In that moment I knew it was entirely possible to orgasm from dirty talk alone. Except it wasn't just dirty talk. Because my heart was flip-flopping in my chest in a weird, terrifying way.

This was just sex. My heart shouldn't…couldn't get involved. No way—

Fear melted into pleasure as his tongue licked me in one long sweep.

Sweet. Heaven.

My eyes rolled as I collapsed onto the bed. He repeated the caress several times, then spread me wider and went to town.

Caleb was a connoisseur, using every part of his mouth on every part of my pussy until I was one delirious mess.

"Please, Caleb," I begged when he drove me to the edge for the umpteenth time, only to withdraw. My fingers speared into his hair, tightening when he started to pull away. "Make me come. *Please, please, please.*"

"Fuck," he groaned against me right before he sucked my clit into his mouth.

I shot off like a rocket, my legs fighting to close as fireworks exploded behind my closed lids. He kept me wide open, working me into a frenzied orgasm that felt like it would last forever.

Convulsions were still rippling through me when I felt him tug on my zipper and remove my dress.

"Caleb," I sighed.

"I'm right here, baby. Hold on." His voice was tight. Edgy.

The sound of ripped foil preceded a hiss from him as he rolled it on; then he crawled over my body. One arm circled my waist, and he tossed me higher up the bed.

"I've been craving this since the moment I saw you," he said, his tongue sliding over one nipple.

My nails dug into his shoulders as fresh waves of pleasure washed over me. "Me, too."

His mouth curved in a smug smile. "How hot were you for me?" The question was rasped against my throat as he grazed my skin with his teeth. He was marking me. I didn't care one little bit.

"Umm…"

He paused and tracked the blush creeping up my neck. "You wanted my cock pounding your pretty little pussy even as you were snapping at me, didn't you?"

I wriggled, half-shamed, half-impatient. "Yes!"

"Don't fret, baby. You're going to get it exactly as you wanted it."

He matched words to action.

With one hand planted next to my head, he trailed the other over my breast, my quivering belly to my pussy. He slid two fingers inside me, his eyes absorbing my reaction. His face tautened at my gasp.

"Please, Caleb, I'm ready. Don't wait."

His teeth gritted, but he continued to fuck me with his fingers, stretching me for another minute before he drew my leg higher, and nudged my entrance with his cock.

Slowly, excruciatingly, he pushed inside me, filling me, stretching me to the point of pain. "God, you're so tight."

He withdrew. Pushed back in. I bit my lip to keep from crying out.

He tensed. "Lily?"

I shook my head. "I'm good."

"You're not good. You're so fucking small," he bit out tersely.

I dug my nails into his back. "Don't stop! Please don't stop." I clamped my legs around him, raised my hips to meet his next thrust. Pain and pleasure collided and I screamed.

"Shit!"

"More," I begged.

A wave of uncertainty flashed across his face. Then it morphed into something else. Something hot and dangerous and guaranteed to send me to another stratosphere. Incredibly, it made me wetter. He felt it on his next thrust when his cock seated deeper inside me.

A mini-roar erupted from his throat. "Jesus, you're incredible."

I hauled myself up on one elbow, fused my mouth to his for a hot moment before dropping back down. "More, please, Caleb."

He didn't need any more begging. He fucked me until my vision blurred and my heart pounded against my rib cage. Until sweat dripped from his body to mine, and my screams mingled with his thick groans.

Until one last series of pounding ripped me from reality and I blacked out from pleasure. I wasn't sure how long I blissed out. But when I resurfaced, he was still a hard, unspent presence inside me.

Tension still gripped him and sweat dotted his upper lip. "Did I tell you how much I love watching you come?" he rasped.

I shook my head, stunned by his control.

"Well, I do. I could watch you all day." He started to move inside me again.

"Oh, God... I can't."

He kissed me, hard and quick. "Wrap your legs around me and give me one more, baby. Just one more."

He caught the heels of my last climax minutes later, unraveling me as he roared his own release. I was fairly sure I passed out again.

When I came to, I was stretched on top of him, his arms clamped around me with his chin resting on top of my head.

My hand trembled as I caressed his chest. "Caleb?"

"Hmm?"

"I... I don't think I can move."

A low, deep laugh rumbled from him. "That's okay. I can't move, either."

A happy little note strummed in my heart, the first warning that I had let in a seemingly harmless virus that could potentially compromise my very existence.

Because as I drifted off to sleep it struck me that I would be totally okay if he didn't move from my bed.

Not tonight.

Not tomorrow.

Not ever.

CHAPTER TWELVE

Caleb

IT WAS SEVEN o'clock and I'd been up for an hour. I should get up. Draw clear lines by returning to my room.

I didn't engage in cozy heart-to-hearts. I never fell asleep in a woman's bed. Or, worse, woke up and... *lingered*.

Yet I couldn't move.

Because I had no clue where the line was anymore. I'd given Lily the green light to blur it, and I'd completely obliterated it by sleeping with her.

And hell, I'd barely scratched the surface of my need for her. I couldn't get enough of Lily. Her silky softness. Her smell. The way her eyelids fluttered as she dreamed.

I breathed out slowly, reluctant to wake her even though my eager dick was raring to go again.

One taste and I was addicted. Enough to remain in her bed, enjoying her slight weight draped over me as I waited for her to wake up so I could indulge all over again.

Despite being more than a little rattled that I'd also experienced the soundest, nightmare-free sleep in years.

The jagged, heart-pounding images that usually taunted me with how I failed to save my mother were so inherent I'd accepted their presence.

Last night they didn't materialize. It was disturbing to even consider that Lily had anything to do with it. That something as simple as sharing bits of our past with each other had achieved this result.

It was absurd, right?

Unbidden, other moments filtered through—her pain during our first lunch in the restaurant. Her tears when she told me about her stepfather. Exposing her vulnerability at the possibility of one of her team sabotaging her work.

After the sort of childhood Lily had experienced, many people would've cut their families out of their lives and closed themselves off.

I was surprised she hadn't.

Stephen Gracen parked himself on his favorite bar stool in his favorite Irish pub most days before noon and stayed till closing, his tab settled courtesy of the money he'd made off his stepdaughter's talent. The guy I sent to Boston to check him out had reported that while Gracen hadn't exactly talked trash about Lily, he hadn't been complimentary, either.

Gracen was either too bitter or too stupid to realize the gem he had in his stepdaughter.

I'd met several Silicon Valley types who thought they were hot shit because they could string code together that baffled the common man.

In the past few days I'd discovered that Lily, despite being a highly intelligent woman who was mostly likely being paid millions for her professional skills, wasn't in any way a pampered princess.

She was caring and considerate.

And she'd shared her deepest pain with me.

Scattered across several events, they'd seemed minor but put together they were huge. Put-your-trust-in-another-person huge.

When was I remotely okay with being that guy?

I eyed the bedroom door, wondering again why I wasn't hightailing out of it.

Because you want the same from her.

The sharp ache in my chest answered the inner voice.

I shifted again, uncomfortable at the fresh turmoil churning inside me.

This was why I didn't do feelings. So far, every encounter between us had come packed with them, even the moments she'd accepted my help to ease her stress sexually. They were all emotional land mines that usually had pushed my eject button.

I gritted my teeth. I liked her. A hell of a lot. But feelings and fucking didn't mix well. Period.

She stirred against me. I looked down and saw her watching me with contemplative eyes. It was that same look she'd given me before prying secrets from me yesterday in the car.

"You look seriously…*serious.*" Wary questions lurked in her eyes, traces of unease and all those pitfalls I suspected came with the morning after a night of earth-shattering sex.

"For a genius, I expected more eloquence than *seriously serious.*" I kept my voice light.

Her hand drifted up my waist to my chest even though her eyes remained dark, searching. "Okay, how about this." Her thigh brushed my hard-on. "Is that one of my sex toys in your lap or are you just extremely happy to see me?"

Sex. This I could handle.

Talking about my mother and how I would have her back in a heartbeat, if only for a chance to do things differently, push harder, shout louder until my voice was heard, until she got the help she needed, I most definitely couldn't.

I smiled past my disquiet, willing my emotions to detach again as I rolled her over and slid two fingers beneath the choker we never got round to taking off last night. "In case I need to spell it out, your battery-operated boyfriends have had their privileges revoked for the foreseeable future. I'm taking care of your every need from now on."

The words echoed with an unnerving sense of permanence, sending another spike of unease up my spine.

Something flitted through her eyes before her lids swept down, cutting me off from her expression. When she looked back up, her eyes contained nothing but hot sexual promise. "If it's going to be anywhere near as good as last night…"

I brushed my lips over hers, teasing even though I wanted to plunge in and devour. "That better not be a challenge, baby. Or I'll be forced to give you a demonstration."

Her breathing picked up, her pulse racing against my fingers. "Yes, please."

Before the words were out of her mouth, I was sliding my tongue between her lips, giving her a vivid taste of what was coming.

A moan rolled from her throat as her fingers dug into my back. My dick jerked, homing in on that place between her open thighs. When her eager wetness greeted it, my vision blurred.

For the first time in my life, I wondered what it would be like to take a woman bare, to glide skin on skin. To come at the gateway to where a new life could be created—

Christ, what the hell is wrong with you?

I dragged my mouth from hers, scrambling for sanity before I did something unthinkable, like ask if she was on the pill. If another man had ever been with her the way I suddenly craved to be.

Irrational jealousy bubbled up, joining the deranged carnival going on inside me. The hand fondling one gorgeous breast tightened.

She inhaled sharply. "Caleb?" Bewilderment laced her lust-soaked voice.

Get yourself together!

I dropped a contrite kiss on her mouth. "Shower or pool?" In the hour before she woke, before perplexing thoughts ruined my mood, I listed all the places I wanted to fuck her.

She blinked, then murmured, "Shower."

Thank fuck. I didn't think I'd make it to the pool.

I scooped her out of bed, grabbed a condom before walking us into the bathroom. Like mine, there was a huge copper roll-top bathtub and a separate shower stall.

I held her against me as I turned on the shower and adjusted the temperature. When my hands slid from her ass to her waist to set her down, the arms around my neck clung, forcing me to look into her face.

"Caleb, are you okay?" she asked, still a little hesitant.

Hell, no, I wasn't. But I wasn't going to attempt to

explain something that puzzled the shit out of me. "You took your time to wake up. I've been rock-hard for you for over an hour," I deflected, cupping her breasts and mercilessly teasing her nipples.

The tactic worked. Her head dropped back and she whimpered. I continued to fondle her as I nudged her against the wall, watched the spray hit her chest and cascade down her body. I'd never seen anything more beautiful.

She made another innocent, dirty sound and I couldn't help but press my mouth against her, gliding my tongue against hers to devour the sound.

My hand slid down her belly, through the trimmed thatch of hair to her sweet, soaked pussy, before inserting two fingers inside her.

Her hand fisted my hair as she gasped.

"Good?" I demanded against her mouth.

"So, so good," she moaned.

I finger-fucked her slow and steady, until her eyes rolled and her thighs shook. Until her cries echoed through the steam.

Only then did I slide on the condom and flip her around. "Brace your hands on the wall and arch your back for me, my dirty little angel."

A smile laced her arousal. "I see you've started with the pet names again."

"I never promised I would stop. Besides, you could lead a man straight to his doom."

She sent me a sultry glance over one shoulder. "Just a man?"

Something bit hard inside me. "Fine. You could lead *me* straight to the gates of hell. Is that what you want to hear?"

Her eyes searched mine. "Maybe."

I hooked one finger into the choker, using the leverage to bring her head back to align her face with mine. "That back still isn't arched. Do I need to spank obedience out of you?" I growled against her throat.

Her whole body shook. Then, with a slow sensual stretch that wouldn't have been amiss on a mermaid, she curved her spine, until her gorgeous twin globes perfectly framed my cock.

I looked down and nearly lost my mind. "God...Lily. You know exactly how to drive me insane, don't you?"

Her answer was to rise on her tiptoes. "Fuck me, Caleb."

With a less than gentle touch, I grabbed her hip and yanked her back onto my waiting cock.

She screamed. My insanity tripled. I forgot to breathe, forgot to think. Forgot everything but the need to bury my cock inside her over and over again.

"Yes. Yes! More," she panted, delirious in her pleasure.

"You're a greedy little thing, aren't you? Always demanding more."

Her fingers clawed the tiles. "Don't stop. Please don't stop."

She continued to beg. I gave her everything until we were seconds from imploding. Then she reached up, covered the hand I had on her choker, locked her eyes on mine and croaked, "Tighter."

A little shocked and a hell of a lot more turned on than I'd ever been in my life, I hooked another finger beneath the tight lace.

She started to come. Endlessly. Gripping me with muscles that demanded my complete surrender. I clung to sanity just so I could watch her for one more soul-shaking second. And holy hell, Lily Gracen, lost in ecstasy, was beyond magnificent.

In that moment before the bottom fell out of my world, I wished I could freeze time. Wished this transcendental moment would never end.

Transcendental. Soul-shaking. *Feelings*.

The next shudder that gripped me had nothing to do with my phenomenal orgasm and everything to do with *emotions* attempting to shift the center of my gravity.

Enough.

The stern warning didn't stop me from kissing her crown and sliding my hand down her back before I pulled out. We both groaned and subsided into silence, words seeming superfluous in this aftermath. I disposed of the condom, turned her around, then directed the flow of water over both of us.

Her eyes were still glazed, but as I reached for the simple lock that secured her choker, her gaze darted to mine.

I froze, waiting for her to speak.

Her nostrils quivered as she sucked in a breath. "I… want you to know…I've never done that before," she muttered. "I was just…"

I brushed my fingers over her lips, absorbing the electric delight that lit through me. "You don't need to explain, sweetheart. If it helps, the effect on you was fantastic for me, too."

A deep blush swept over her cheeks as she caught my hand in hers and kissed my knuckles.

The move was unexpectedly sweet. For a split second, I wanted to succumb.

I returned to my task and undid the choker. Red

marks ringed her neck, a perfect imprint of the lace pattern. I trailed my lips over the mark, still caught in the cycle I couldn't break free from, feeling a little perverse that the sight of it aroused me.

The gel I picked up smelled like Lily. I washed her from head to toe, lingering in places that made her gasp.

Then she held out her hand for the bottle. I handed it over and braced my palms over the wall above her head. I was hard again before she was halfway down my chest.

I didn't reach for her. I needed a moment to regroup, to make sure I could emerge from whatever was happening between us with my faculties intact. When she sank onto her knees, I squeezed my eyes shut and locked my jaw as her small, wicked fingers washed my cock, my balls, then finally moved lower.

I was so focused on not grabbing her for another mind-blowing fuck, I didn't realize she'd ducked under my arm to wash my back until she gasped.

Shit. The scar.

Gentle fingers touched my left shoulder blade where the bullet grazed me. "What happened?"

Her soft sympathy reached inside me, further weakening rigid foundations. My shrug didn't hit the offhand mark as I turned. "Trigger-happy client. Let's get out of here and I'll tell you the full story over breakfast."

She looked disappointed but she didn't say anything as I rinsed off and grabbed a towel. In the bedroom I gathered my clothes, aware that her gaze grew more guarded with each passing second.

I tightened my gut against the urge to reassure her. It was better this way. I wasn't about to break open a box of hearts and flowers. Even if I once possessed such a box it had been smashed beneath the reality of repeated promises made and broken with callous indifference. Every single promise made to help my mother had been broken.

Then Kirsten came along and drove the knife in deeper.

I wasn't about to speak words I didn't mean or give reassurance that I couldn't back up. "I'll see you downstairs in ten?"

She blinked, then jerked out a nod.

I walked out, suspecting that the word *bastard* was lit up in Lily's mind right now. I slammed the door in my room, then stood frozen in place. Could I have handled it better?

No. Maybe. Minutes ticked by, then I heard her walk past my door.

Fuck it. I threw on fresh clothes with an urgency I didn't understand, and rushed downstairs to find Lily hovering by the front door wearing a tight black T-shirt that ended where a pair of leather shorts started. Those shorts ended at the top of her thighs, leaving an indecent amount of leg showing. She wore minimal makeup, but her eyes were darkly outlined, and her lips gleamed a faint pink. The wrist cuffs were back in place, as was a new, broader choker.

God, if she was trying to torture me, it was working. She looked phenomenal.

I swallowed my tongue, spotted the keys in her hand and realized she was dressed for *outside*.

"Where are you going?"

Her chin lifted. "For breakfast. Where else?"

"Lily—"

"Oh, and I'm driving this time." She twirled the keys. "You can come with me or you can follow me."

My jeans and T-shirt were okay to go out but I would've followed regardless. She stepped outside and hurried to the garage.

"Lily, let's talk about this—"

"Let's not," she snapped. "And if you even *think* about physically restraining me, I'll rip your balls off."

I believed her. But I still shook my head as I followed her to the garage. "No can do, baby. I catch the smallest sign of danger and I'm getting *very* physical. Count on it."

I let her glare at me for a full five seconds before opening the Mini's door for her. She slid behind the wheel. Going around I said a prayer and contorted myself into the passenger seat.

She drove fast without breaking limits and considerately without being a pushover. Me, she completely ignored. We passed several respectable cafés before she stopped at an upmarket bistro. She surprised me by bypassing the parking lot and heading for the drive-through lane. It wasn't your average drive-through. Shiny food trucks displayed glorious baked goods, bacon, cheeses and everything in between.

Two guys and a woman manned the trucks. The woman smiled when she spotted Lily. "Hey, girl." She handed over two big paper bags with the bistro's logo on it.

"Thanks," Lily replied.

I deposited the bags on the backseat and reached for my wallet, but she was already driving away.

In between ensuring I wasn't blocking the blood flow to my legs and trying not to drool over her legs, I decided to maintain silence. Ten minutes later she pulled up to an abandoned lot with a tall wall erected on the south edge. She drove to the center, stopped next to a bench and turned off the engine.

I stepped out with our food and looked around. "What's this place?" I asked.

"It used to be a drive-in theater." She reached into the bag and started setting out the food. Bacon. Bagels. Cream cheese. Coffee.

I had zero appetite but I accepted the coffee. She laced hers with cream and sugar, took a sip and set it back down.

"Who owns this place?"

"For now, the original owner. Next month, maybe me."

I nodded at the food. "Why the drive-through? Why here?"

She stared into her coffee. Then shrugged. "Your guys didn't have a chance to check out the bistro first. And I knew I could be alone here."

I. Not *we.*

I waited a beat. "You're pissed."

Her mouth firmed. "Give the man a prize."

My jaw clenched. "Enough. You've made your point with your little tantrum."

Anger flashed across her face. I watched her rein it in. "Fine. Talk to me, then, Caleb. Convince me I didn't just sleep with an asshole who couldn't even be bothered with conversation after he fucked me."

"Jesus…"

"Leave him out of it. This is between you and me."

Absurdly, I wanted to smile. But her beautiful face was a picture of hurt she was trying to hide. I dragged a hand down my stubbled face. "Full confession. What we did kinda…blew my mind."

Shock replaced hurt, and then her expression slowly softened. After a minute she nodded. "Me, too," she whispered, blushing fiercely.

"Okay. Now that we've got that squared away, how can I make you feel…less pissed?"

She grabbed a sliced bagel, tore a piece, but didn't eat it. "I want to know you, Caleb. Tell me something."

I took a deep breath. "You know I grew up on the rough streets of LA."

Her hand trembled as she stared wide-eyed at me. "Yes. Was it after you lost your mom?"

Christ. I weighed the option of evasion against the return of her hurt, and grimaced inwardly. "It was before. And after. She was a manic-depressive. The moments of light in her darkness were very few but for the first nine years of my life she had medical insurance and a decent doctor to prescribe her the right medication."

"Caleb—"

My fingers brushed her lips, silencing her. "I don't like telling this story. Let me tell it once and be done. Okay?"

A small nod.

My chest tightened as memories flooded in. "She lost her job and the domino effect of no insurance, losing our house, ending up at a halfway house, then a shelter, sent her into a deeper hole. I was eleven before we were assigned a place in Trenton Gardens."

Lily winced but I couldn't let her sympathy affect me.

"But it was too late. She'd lost the will to…" I took a breath. "I was the only thing she fought for. Every time social services tried to take me away, she would fight to keep me. I've no idea how she did it, but she won. But then she would spiral back into darkness. I couldn't help her. I called every helpline I could find, wrote a dozen letters every week to anyone I thought could help. The doctors we managed to see were hopeless. Twice, she tried to end her life. Every time they sent her home from the hospital with a damn leaflet. I even pawned her jewelry to pay for an appointment with a private doctor. The pills he prescribed helped. When she ran out I called my social worker and asked her to help me get her more. She just…laughed at me." Anger and despair I hadn't felt in a long time swelled inside me. I withdrew my hand from Lily's, clenched it in my lap and took another breath. "Anyway, she succeeded on her third attempt."

"Oh, God…"

Tears spilled down her cheeks. I opened my mouth to tell her not to cry for me. Then stopped. I *wanted* her soft sympathy. It was a salve to a wound that had never healed. Shedding tears for my mother was one of the many things I hadn't been able to do for her. Maybe Lily's tears would be enough to let her know how sorry I was for failing.

Lily got up, walked round and slid into my lap. "I'm so sorry." Her arms circled my neck. I hugged her close, breathed in her goodness. And just like in the bathroom, I never wanted this moment to end.

I never wanted to let her go.

Which was crazy. We'd only known each other for a week. And…dammit, I didn't do feelings!

I looked around and grimaced. "Can we continue this at home?" I said, raising my eyebrow.

For some reason my cocked eyebrow made her smile. "Too wide-open-spaces for you?"

"Something like that," I said, looking down at the table. "Breakfast is ruined, though."

She shrugged. "I wasn't that hungry anyway."

I scowled. "A woeful waste of good bacon."

Her smile widened as she stood up. "We have bacon at home," she suggested.

Unable to keep my hands off her, I grabbed her and trailed my hands up her thighs. "Is there an offer in there?"

Her fingers tunneled through my hair, gently massaging my scalp. "If you want. But I don't break out my culinary skills for just anyone."

I caught a trace of pain through the flippant words. "Why not?"

Green eyes darted away, then came back. "Stepdaddy issues. In return for him…tolerating me, I had to cook for him. It made me hate cooking."

I caressed her damp cheek. "He doesn't deserve your love. Or your pain."

Her eyes misted. "It's not easy to brush it off."

True. I'd lived with guilt and anger for so long it was fused into my DNA. "I get it."

"Caleb?"

"Yeah."

"I was thinking…maybe your presence has achieved the opposite of what we hoped. Maybe instead of bringing my stalker out into the open, he's given up?"

"Sorry to disappoint you, but assholes like that don't go away easily. I'm close to catching him. Trust me. Okay?"

Small, soft hands framed my face. "Okay."

My hands coasted higher, brushed the underside of her breasts. Her breathing altered. "Let's go home."

She nodded.

We threw the uneaten breakfast in the trash. I winced as I folded myself back into the car. "This is the second thing I'm punishing you for when we get back."

Her eyes widened. "What's the first thing?"

"Driving me insane with those fucking shorts," I griped, reaching down to adjust my hard-on. "That was the intention, wasn't it?"

Pink flared in her cheeks. "Maybe."

"Well, you are *definitely* getting your ass spanked for it."

Hot anticipation washed away the last of the sadness and pain in her eyes.

When she pulled up at a stop sign, I dragged my gaze from her slim thighs to her face, then her hair. "Has your hair always been this color?"

She shook her head. "It used to be dark blond." She grabbed a lock at her right temple. "This part started turning whiter when I was twelve. It was cool at first. Then I got tired of it. So I went white all over."

"I like it. A lot."

Her gaze latched on to mine. We stared at one another, pure electricity zinging between us. The driver behind us honked impatiently. She jumped, then laughed. Her laughter triggered mine, easing the tension of the past hour. The lightness stayed as we drove through the gates. As I threw her over my shoulder and rushed through the front door into the living room.

Maybe this…unburdening thing wasn't catastrophic after all.

Maybe breaking my rule for her wasn't the end of the world.

Maybe—

We froze as the TV flicked to life of its own accord. Except that was impossible. Not without electronic intervention.

That intervention arrived in the form of neon green bits of code raining down the screen, then a masked face framed by a black hoodie. I pushed Lily behind me as if it would protect her from the loud, distorted voice that filled the room.

"Hello, Lily Gracen. First of all, congratulations. You're very close to achieving perfection with your code. Don't be frightened. I represent interested parties wishing to form a partnership. Apologies if I've made you a little…uncomfortable lately. But I urge you not to give the code to SDM or I'll have no choice but to stay in your life a while longer. Think about it. I'll be in touch. Oh, and tell that fixer to go home to LA. He won't be of much use to you."

The strangled sound Lily made cut to the heart of me. I took a step toward the TV just as it went blank.

A loud pop shot through the house, then an eerie silence echoed in its wake.

CHAPTER THIRTEEN

Caleb

"WHAT ARE YOU DOING?"

"We're getting the hell out of here." I spotted an overnight bag and handed it to her. "Pack what you need but do it fast."

She reached for my hand. "Caleb—"

I turned away, fist clenched, the need to punch something running wild through me. "Lily, the asshole hacked your Wi-Fi, sent the transmission, then hit the house with an electromagnetic wave that killed the electricity on the whole street. You're not staying here. Not until I have my hands around his fucking throat."

To her credit, she didn't dawdle. She stuffed clothes into the bag, added essentials, then grabbed her satchel and purse.

Ten minutes later we were driving away from the house.

"Your guys searched the area. Did they find anything?"

My security team's presence had provided some reassurance, but not enough to close the horrified black chasm in my stomach at the thought that from the moment we returned to the house, we were sitting ducks. It snatched my breath. Reminded me of the consequences of dropping my guard.

"Caleb?"

I gathered my scattered thoughts. "They found motorcycle tracks behind the house."

She flinched at my cold tone, but said nothing for a couple of miles. "Where are we going?"

"To the airport."

"And then?"

"We're swinging by my place in Malibu. Then I'm taking you to the safe house in Lake Tahoe." I should've done that in the first place. Regardless of the fact that bringing her home had produced the desired effect of drawing the stalker out, the flip side was much worse. The EMP blast could've been knockout gas. Or—

"So you still don't know who it is?"

My fingers tightened on the wheel. "No."

She didn't speak much after that. Neither did I. I was too busy playing worst-case-scenario.

Anything could've happened to Lily.

My jet was ready when we arrived at the airport. We took off immediately. Leaving Lily in the club chair upfront, I retreated to the back of the plane and dialed Maggie.

She answered on the first ring. "Boss, how can I help?"

"I've left three guys in Palo Alto to track down this bastard. I need another team at the Reno safe house."

"I'll get right on it."

I hung up, then went through my contacts. Every favor owed to me, I shamelessly called on. By the time we landed in LA I was in a better frame of mind.

My house in Malibu was set on a bluff that over-looked a private beach. The helipad that came with the property had been used only a handful of times. Today it came in handy as a way of avoiding LA's hor-rendous traffic.

I walked in and my steps slowed. The last time I was here I was in complete control of my world, my only focus on being bigger, better, *badder*.

In the space of seven days, the ground had shifted beneath me, attempted to change my orbit. All because of the stunning woman who stopped beside me, her eyes lighting on the space I'd claimed, possessions that pro-claimed my success. That fierce yearning to hang on to her clobbered me again. I smashed it to pieces.

No more breaking rules.

"Hang tight. I'll be right back." I sprinted upstairs to my bedroom to retrieve the weapons I kept in the safe.

I came down to find her at the window, staring at the ocean with her arms wrapped around her middle. She turned at my approach. "Can't we just stay here?"

The urge to say yes pounded me. "No. This place is secure enough but it's in my name. Any fucker with a computer can find it. I need you off the grid."

Resigned, she nodded.

We headed outside and reboarded the chopper.

"Chance will need to know I'm going off-grid."

My teeth gritted. "No, he doesn't. You still have time before your deadline. And frankly, I don't want him anywhere near you right now."

Again, she didn't react as expected. She was either in shock or afraid. Neither of the two sat well with me.

"Lily…"

Her fingers curled in her lap. "What if it's someone close to me? What would that say about my judgment?"

"You're not blaming yourself for this." That ball was squarely in my court.

"Since you don't know *who* it is, that's easier said than done," she murmured.

I had no answer to that so I remained silent as we reboarded the plane and took off.

There was very little in the way of conversation during the flight.

Many times I opened my mouth to say something, then decided against it.

Action, not platitudes.

Maggie had lined up another SUV for us, and I high-tailed it out of the airport with one eye on the police scanner on the dashboard. I wanted to get us to the cabin on the Nevada side of the lake as quickly as possible without attracting attention from the cops for speeding.

Twenty minutes later I breathed a sigh of relief when I spotted the turnoff for the dirt track leading to the cabin. I'd kept it overgrown on purpose. There were no signposts or no trespassing warnings to attract inquisitive neighbors.

The Jeffrey pines lining the track and surrounding the property were ideal for mounting security cameras and other intruder-warning triggers.

I pulled up in front of the cabin in Knots Peak, killed the engine and glanced over at Lily. She was staring at the log building that would be her home until I came through with my assurance to catch her stalker.

My gaze slid past her to the three-leveled property. The one-bedroom dilapidated structure I bought five years ago had been expanded into a no-cost-spared piece of real estate worth ten times its original price.

It was one of three safe houses I owned around the country. The other four were overseas but this was my favorite. On the rare occasion I took downtime from fixing other people's problems, the cabin was my first choice.

There would be no downtime, though. I'd dropped my guard, messed around with a client and the bastard had gotten close.

Fury and guilt bubbled inside as I threw open the door. "Let's get you inside."

I grabbed her bag and walked her to the front door. A palm print and alphanumeric code released the lock.

Rugs spread out in the wide hallway and over polished wooden floors throughout the cabin muffled our footsteps. Exposed oak beams propped up high ceilings in the living room, and light filtered in from a wide window facing the lake.

I stashed her bag in the bedroom before returning to the living room. Still clutching her satchel, she stood at the window, lost in the view.

"The window is one-way glass so no one can see inside. Even at night you'll be able to see the lake. That should help a little." Shit, I sounded like a damn realtor.

She turned, wary eyes catching mine. "Help with what?"

I shrugged. "Not everyone likes being stuck in the middle of nowhere. The lake will give you something to look at."

"I'm okay with it," she replied, although her sleek white throat moved in a nervous swallow. I dragged my gaze away from the smooth landscape of her skin. Giving in to those insane yearnings was what had landed us here.

"Good. Security-wise, the outer doors are made of solid oak. It would take a very large ax or a sizeable explosive device to breach it. The woods for half a mile radius are part of the property. There are a few booby traps to prevent intruders."

She frowned. "What kinds of traps?"

"Very effective ones," I gritted out, partly to reassure her, partly to reassure myself.

She flinched; then her lips pursed.

I dragged my hands down my face and walked over to her. Every cell in my body was dying to touch her. But I'd already let too much *personal* get in the way.

It was time to revert to Caleb Steele, Stone-Cold Fixer.

Jaw set, I moved toward the French doors. "I need to go through the cabin's security with you. Familiarize yourself with the property."

"Why are you being so cold?"

Her soft, bewildered words were like a punch to the gut. I steeled myself against it before turning to face her.

"You wanted to know what happened to my shoulder? I got involved with a client. Kirsten was an actress, one of my first clients. She'd made a couple of wrong choices in the past. The studio she was working with was threatening to fire her over some revealing pictures. She begged me to help. She was beautiful and I was young, foolish and…into her." Lily's gaze dropped and a look I couldn't fathom crossed her face. "When she needed a car, I gave her mine. When she needed a place to stay, I asked her to move in with me." My bitter laughter seared my throat. "Hell, I believed we were in a *relationship*. Right up until I found her banging the director. Even then I thought she was the victim. I punched his lights out and caused general mayhem that ensured my fledgling career tanked before it'd taken off properly. And Kirsten's response? She went off her head because I'd just ruined her chances for another movie and decided she didn't want me in her life after all so she tried to fucking shoot me."

Lily blanched. "Oh, my God!"

I shrugged despite the fury of bitterness and anger dueling inside me. "Luckily, she was a very lousy shot. Anyway, if it hadn't been for Ross's father, I'd still be fixing problems for gangsters back in Trenton Gardens. He gave me a piece of advice, one I'd already figured out the hard way—never get involved with a client."

A horrified little sound escaped her throat, scraping on my nerve endings. "S-so you think this is my fault?" she whispered.

I opened my mouth to say *hell, no*, but then stopped. She was partly to blame. She'd gotten under my skin with her soft sympathy and her flashes of innocence and her incredible inner strength in the face of adversity and her gloriously tight body. Even now, she continued to drive me insane with her jaw-dropping beauty.

"I think my point has been proven conclusively that shit happens when you break the rules," I said. "Besides, you were on a mission of your own, weren't you?"

She gasped and her eyes darkened in pain. I turned away. My point was made. And I still had a stalker to catch.

"Security tour. Now." I crossed to the French doors on the other side of the living room and stepped out onto the porch, not looking back to see if she was following.

The sky was a clear blue, and the cool air was drifting in from the lake. It was all so fucking idyllic.

When I heard her behind me, I went down wooden stairs leading to a sloping garden. A staggered limestone feature tumbled water into the rock pond one level lower and stopped next to a covered hot tub. I bypassed it, trying not to think of Lily immersed in the swirling bubbles, completely naked, with the setting sun gleaming on her glorious skin.

A few hours ago I would've said, *forget the fucking tour, let's go to bed.* But my sex-addled brain had put her in danger.

We skirted the garden and the high stone walls to stop at the side gate. "This leads down to the lake. And a boat for a quick getaway if you need to. The code is 40998061."

Fear sparked through the shadowed swirls in her eyes. I forced myself not to react to it.

After a few beats she placed her thumb against the panel, and the gate sprang open. The scent of pine and earth grew as we stepped onto the uneven path and walked in silence to the jetty. "Have you driven a boat before?"

"No."

"The keys are hidden beneath the sixth slab…right here." I tried to ignore the feel of her silky skin as I caught her arm and pointed to the wooden plank. "It's screwed in but loose enough to pry apart in a hurry if you need to."

The boat was a few years old but was kept in good condition and fully fueled at all times.

She hopped down before I could help her, and then took a step away from me. I gritted my teeth against the grating discomfort in my chest and pointed to the ignition. "Twist to the left and hold. Engine should kick in. Then push the lever. Ignore everything else."

"It looks pretty straightforward."

"It might not be if you're panicking," I bit out.

Her cheeks lost color, but she nodded. "Understood."

We returned to the house and I took her round the lower level to another door. "Same code as the gate but backward."

"16089904," she repeated instantly.

Hell, even scrambling to maintain distance, I couldn't help but admire her incredible brain.

The large room that doubled up as a games room and gym took up most of the square footage of the cabin. It was also self-contained enough to use as a sleeping place for the odd bodyguard or two when needed.

I bypassed the doors connecting the short hallway to the stairs leading up and headed to the far wall. When she joined me, I pushed on the fourth wooden panel. A five-foot partition sprang open to reveal a small spiral staircase. "This takes you straight up into the kitchen. After you."

She sprinted up lithely on the balls of her feet. I took the stairs much slower, unable to take my eyes off the ass that'd cradled my cock in the shower this morning.

Her steps slowed as she neared the top.

"Is there a problem?" The question emerged with a tight croak.

I stopped two steps below her, keeping us at eye level. Close enough for me to lean forward and taste the sinfully gorgeous mouth currently pinched with tension. I locked my knees hard and reminded myself that my wayward cock had brought us to this.

"You didn't bring in your bag from the car. And you've just given me a very detailed tour. Why?"

Chains shackled my chest. "Because I'm returning to Palo Alto."

"You're leaving." The statement was final and chilled.

Unaccustomed dread slowly filled my chest.

I'd pushed her into accepting that what happened with us was a mistake, and yet seeing that acceptance in her eyes had lodged a cold, hard ball in my gut.

I braced a hand against the banister as another truth bit me hard. I'd told her to *trust me*. And had done zero to back it up.

My failures, rehashed just a few short hours ago, slashed me in half.

Bitter laughter seared my throat as patterns were laid bare.

My success rate with jobs that didn't require emotional expenditure was near perfect. Those I allowed myself to care about were doomed to failure. My mother. Then Kirsten. Now Lily.

And yes…I cared about Lily. Hell, I was damned sure *caring* was too mild a word for it.

I gathered every last scrap of emotion, knotted it into a cold ball, and buried it deep. Then I forced a nod, despite my veins beginning to fill with icy water. "I can't find your stalker stuck here with you. I need to get back, rattle a few cages."

Her eyes, no longer that gorgeous shade of green I loved, shadowed even further. Then she gathered that admirable strength and nodded. "I see. You better get to it then."

Something that tasted uncannily like anguish billowed up from my feet to lodge in my throat. No amount of bracing myself could prevent it saturating every corner of my being as I watched her walk to the sofa and snatch up her satchel.

"Lily." I said her name for the simple, selfish reason that I couldn't bear the distance between us.

She glanced impatiently at me. "What?"

I pointed to the fridge. "You didn't have any breakfast. You need to eat something."

Her gaze swung blankly to the fridge. Then she frowned. "I'm not hungry."

"Well, eat anyway. You'll need—"

"I'm not a child. I'm capable of feeding myself when I need to, thanks."

I opened my mouth. My phone beeped. I read the message and my heart sank.

Me, the man of action who abhorred drawn-out goodbyes, was reeling that his time was up with Lily Gracen. "Your security team is here."

She nodded stiffly as I introduced her to her three minders. Two disappeared to take up positions around the perimeter. The one tasked to stay inside with her at all times retreated to a respectful distance.

"Was there anything else?" she asked coldly.

There were a thousand things. But everything started and ended with the fact that I'd failed her. So not a single word emerged.

Slowly her eyes grew colder, her face a mask of disappointment as she strutted to the door and pointedly threw it open.

"Goodbye, Caleb." The echoing finality behind her words stayed with me long after my plane soared into the sky, racing me away from her.

CHAPTER FOURTEEN

Lily

HE WAS GONE.

Forty-eight hours later I still couldn't believe how quickly everything had turned to ash. When Maggie called last night to ask if I needed anything, I had to bite my tongue hard to stop myself from asking about Caleb.

What good would it have done? He blamed me for pushing him into territory he'd never wanted to revisit. And he was right. I'd taken advantage of our insane chemistry just so I could prove I was in control. And I was the one bleeding with no end of the ravaging pain in sight.

The truth wasn't hard to accept. The pain that came with it was.

I'd allowed myself to hope. To care.

If only I hadn't let the moments of gentleness and protectiveness weave into my heart. If only he hadn't opened up at the drive-in…

If only the phenomenal sex hadn't left me raw and reeling and craving the impossible.

From the start he'd made it clear sex was off the

table as long as I was his client. And I'd seen that as a challenge.

Misery clawed through me. My heart shuddered and I blinked to stop the fierce prickling that preceded tears.

God, was it even possible to fall in love in seven short days?

My inability to catch my breath, the endless turmoil in my mind and the anguish coursing through my body, screamed *yes*. Butting heads with him at the start had been my mating dance. Giving him my body had gone hand in hand with giving him my heart. A heart left battered even before it'd had a chance to soar.

If I had to pinpoint when it was well and truly doomed, it was the moment he confirmed why he became a fixer.

I couldn't even hate him for that. He'd never hidden himself from me.

Maybe it was better this way. Having happiness snatched from me before I truly tasted it would be a blessing somewhere down the road.

I stared at the horizon, watching the fingers of dawn trail the inky blue sky. Down by the water I spotted Kurt, the minder who'd pulled lake duty. I didn't sleep a wink last night. Surprise. But I managed to snatch moments of lucidity, long enough to confirm that it was Sanjeet's code that sabotaged the beta test.

Further anguish weighted my heart, but I was thankful I didn't have to deal with him just yet. I would repair the code on my own and test it vigorously before the next meeting.

Because now more than ever, I needed total control of my life. I had a feeling I'd need it because this ravaging pain wasn't done with me by a long stretch.

Caleb

I jerked awake from a sleep filled with alternating images of losing my mother, then Lily. As I watched, screaming, their images blended, then drifted farther and farther out of reach.

I dragged myself upright to a sweat-soaked T-shirt and guilt-laden relief that immediately morphed into pain.

It'd been like this for the last four interminable days.

In the cold light of day, I could distract myself with something else, although success in that area was dwindling. But in my dreams I was helpless against the savage craving; helpless to fight the powerful emotions that poured out of my soul, wrenched me from sleep only to mock me with the emptiness of my reality.

I stared out the window of the cabin's guest room, the peace I usually found here shattered.

Why the hell did I put her in my bedroom?

So you can torture yourself with visions of her when she's gone, why else?

Perversely, the thought that I'd have *something* to hang on to soothed me a little.

Jesus.

I rose, changed my T-shirt, added sweatpants and grabbed my phone. As I approached the door, my heart began to race.

I told myself the smell of coffee didn't mean a thing. Lack of sleep and the couple of drinks I had on the plane equaled a foggy brain. I could've set the coffee machine myself when I rolled in at…whatever o'clock.

I entered the living room, saw her, and thoughts of time dissolved.

She sat cross-legged on the sofa nearest the window, beneath the worshipful rays of the morning sun.

The leather and lace comprising her usual work attire had been swapped for a less dramatic getup of black T-shirt and jersey shorts. But a choker still circled her neck, cuffs binding her wrists.

She hadn't seen me yet. I needed an uninterrupted minute to imprint her on my memory. Some of the things I said couldn't be taken back.

Hell, my behavior had been beyond shitty. So yeah, the chances of her being gone by nightfall were extremely high.

But God, I needed another minute, because I'd missed her beautiful face…her body…so damn much.

She was spectacular, if elusive, in my dreams but the reality was infinitely better. I approached, the contrasting black-and-white vision of her a magnet I couldn't resist.

She was completely absorbed in her work, her fingers dancing in a hypnotic blur over the keyboard. Earbuds firmly in place cut her off from me.

But then, greedily, I wanted those beautiful green eyes that had invaded my dreams every night since I left on me.

As if she heard my thoughts, her fingers froze.

Her head snapped up, her eyes widened, then dimmed. Her resting expression was a punch in the gut. I tried to absorb it as I strolled closer.

"Hey." She eyed me warily as she plucked her earbuds out. "I didn't…when did you get back?"

"Very late. Or very early."

Her eyes grew more guarded. "Is…everything all right?"

I hesitated.

The moment I answered, it was over. There would be nothing keeping her here. A shamefully large part of me wanted to stall, like I'd wanted to freeze time in the shower, and at the drive-in. Hell, every moment with Lily deserved to be preserved in amber.

But the universe selfishly ticked forward. Gritting my teeth, I indicated the sofa. "May I sit?"

She stared blankly at me, then down at the space before shrugging. "It's your house, Caleb." Her voice was a chilled rasp.

I ignored the ache sucking oxygen out of my lungs and sat down. When she tensed and tucked her legs firmer beneath her, I bunched my fist on my thigh.

Wow, you blew it good this time, Steele.

"Caleb?" Her fingers were curled tensely around the lid of her laptop.

I cleared my throat and fired up the video app on my phone. In a dark gray room, across a desk and two chairs, two men faced each other.

I pointed to the younger man. "Do you know him?"

She set her laptop aside. "No. Should I?"

"His name is Eric Vasiliev. He works for Baitlin Tech."

She blinked. "Baitlin was on the list I gave you."

I nodded. "He's also Sanjeet's roommate."

Alarm widened her eyes. "Okay. Who's the other guy?"

"A friend of mine. He's in law enforcement. He did me a solid."

"How?"

"He interviewed the remaining people on the list, helped me fill out a few blanks."

Her breath caught, hope filling her eyes. "Are you saying... Have you caught my stalker?"

I smiled. "Yes. You don't need to worry. They're in custody. And your algorithm is safe."

Relief drenched her face. She covered her open mouth with one hand. "Oh, my God," she whispered.

I wanted to touch her so badly my hand burned with the need.

She took a few more breaths, and then her gaze returned to the screen. "Did Sanjeet have anything to do with it?"

"Not directly. But he unwittingly started the whole thing. Eric saw what he was working on during a FaceTime call and asked a few questions, enough to get an idea of what you were working on."

"But Sanjeet was just a third of the team, and the others didn't know about each other."

I hit the second video in the folder. "They didn't, but she did."

Lily stared at the video, hurt and anger flashing across her face. "Miranda?"

"Yeah. She had access to you. All she had to do was listen and watch and tell Eric when to strike."

"But...why?"

The throb of anguish in her voice cut through me. I wanted to absorb her pain. "Money. She was dating Eric. They hatched the plan together. All they had to do was destabilize the team, stalk you in the hopes of you making a mistake. If that didn't work they were going to move to outright blackmail to get the code. They had a bidding war going with six countries."

"She told your friend all of this?"

I nodded. "We got it all on tape."

"Oh, my God." Her eyes filled with tears.

Unable to hold back my need, I reached for her. She flinched away, jumped to her feet and paced to the window.

I threw my phone on the coffee table, swallowing the boulder of pain in my throat.

After a minute she swiped her eyes. When she faced me, her face was a controlled mask. "So it's over. I can leave?"

Every ounce of power concentrated in keeping my jaw clenched just so I didn't have to answer. But the part of me that yearned to give her what she wanted forced my head to nod. "The police will need a statement from you at some point, but with the confession they have it should all be straightforward."

Then, unable to sit still, I surged to my feet. "Lily—"

"I want to leave. Now. Please."

No. *Hell, no.*

One look at her face showed my firecracker was back, ready to rain fire and brimstone on me if I didn't grant her wish.

"Lily, we need to talk."

She shook her head. "I need to pack." She darted down the hallway so fast she was a blur.

I followed because, fuck it, I was tired of feeling like shit.

I knocked. At her silence, I entered. She was holding a top, staring blindly into her suitcase. I took another moment to memorize her face.

Her head snapped up, and her face tightened. "What do you want, Caleb? We said everything that needed saying last time."

"No we didn't. I have more to say."

She looked mutinous for a moment, and then her cute chin lifted. "Fine, let's hear it."

My fists tightened, the magnitude of my need an overwhelming weight pressing me down. But I pushed ahead. "I don't want you to leave. We're not done. Hell, we barely even started. I want you back."

A look flashed through her eyes but it was gone too quickly to read. "Wanting me back suggests you had me in the first place. Did you?" she queried almost carelessly.

"What?"

She threw the top into the suitcase. "Let's forget that for a minute. You want me…back…for how long?"

I frowned. "Lily—"

"A week? A month? Two months?"

I shrugged. "It's something we can figure out together."

She laughed, an acid-tipped sound that whipped blades through me. "How? What criteria would you use? When the sex isn't so hot anymore? When your next exciting case came up?"

"If you want a time frame I'm not going to give you one," I snapped with more heat than I'd intended.

She paled. I reached out. She flinched. This wasn't how I'd intended it to go. At all.

"Lily, I—"

"Why did you become a fixer, Caleb?" The question walloped me from left field. Her voice was wooden but her sharp eyes were prying beneath my veneer.

I didn't want to be analyzed. Not while this rawness lived inside me. "Why the hell not?" I snapped again.

"That's not an answer. Shall I tell you what I think? You enjoy the control it gives you. But more than that you enjoy the transient nature of your work. You don't have to invest in the long-term. You go in, all guns blazing, you fix whatever's wrong. And then you *leave*. Don't you?"

I stared at her, trying to summon fury and detachment. All I achieved was a widening of the chasm between us. Fuck it. "Yes," I threw out.

It was the truth, after all.

She whirled to face the window, then almost immediately turned back again. "Well, there's your answer. You can't guarantee anything beyond your next *fix*. That's what you live for. That's all you'll ever care about. But you know what else you can't guarantee? That your neat record will hold out. Sooner or later you'll have to accept that some things can't be fixed."

The raw ache intensified. "What the fuck are you talking about?"

She sighed. "It doesn't matter. I just know that I don't want to be your next fix, Caleb."

Somewhere beneath the roaring in my ears, I heard the sound of her suitcase zipper and the echo of her footsteps down the hallway.

Moments later an engine started, revved, then slowly faded away.

CHAPTER FIFTEEN

Caleb
One month later

"WHY ISN'T THE Landon file on my desk? I asked for it twenty minutes ago. What's going on?" I snarled as Maggie hurriedly slammed her laptop shut.

"Nothing!"

I eyed her, the irritation that had been living beneath my skin for weeks threatening to erupt. "If you want to watch porn, do it in your own time, not on company property. And seriously, I thought you were a much better liar than that?"

"Okay, first of all, ewww. Second of all, double ewww!"

"You have five seconds to fess up before I fire you for inappropriate use of office property."

With a long-suffering sigh, she opened her laptop, and hit Play.

The sweet, sexy voice that lived in my dreams flowed through the speaker. Heart lodged in my throat, I rounded Maggie's desk.

And there she was.

Lily. Giving another interview.

I'd taken pains to avoid all forms of tech news since she left me in Lake Tahoe.

I tried to summon the anger I'd carried with me since she walked out. All I managed was the ashen aftertaste of a poorly handled situation.

I don't want to be your next fix...

I snorted under my breath. Lily Gracen had proven that she was one long fix, one I couldn't get away from whether I was awake or asleep.

She'd burrowed herself firmly beneath my skin, made it so I couldn't take three steps before she crossed my mind. I wasn't sure whether to be pissed with her or feel sorry for myself for allowing her close.

Some things can't be fixed...

Ironically, in letting her smudge the lines, she'd forced me to redraw my rigid boundaries, forced me to examine the hard chains I'd wrapped around myself since my mother died. A few had been rusty, surprisingly easy to break, letting me breathe easier than I had in a very long time.

Some others not so much.

All in all, she'd forced me to examine far too much. Which was why I was still leaning heavily in the pissed column.

And there she was, without a fucking care in the world.

Stunning in customary black. With…a pair of stylish, boxy glasses perched on her nose.

Holy fuck.

That last day in Silicon Valley, sitting in the passenger seat of her cramped-as-hell little car, watching her laugh while wearing those saucy shorts, I thought she couldn't get any more sensational.

I just discovered she could.

"Umm...boss?"

I scowled. "What?"

"Just checking that you're breathing, is all."

I wrenched my gaze from the screen. "I'm not paying you to sit around watching online videos all day, Maggie."

She nodded sagely. "Then I guess you won't want the thing I just sent to your phone."

My scowl deepened. "What thing?" I pulled my phone from my pocket.

It was an invitation to a black tie event. Hosted by SDM. Five thousand dollars a plate. Starting at 8 pm. Tonight.

A tremble rolled up my arm and down my body. "Why the hell did you send me this?"

"Because I'm terrified one of these days you'll develop actual fangs and claws and all my parents will find when they come looking for me is a dried up husk."

"Trust me. If I turned feral you wouldn't be my first choice of a meal."

I knew someone who tasted sweeter. Glorious, in fact. Someone whose every breath I would die for, given half a chance.

"Fine, but just FYI, this is her last gig for SDM. Who knows where she'll disappear to afterward?"

The words struck pure dread into my heart, pissing me off even more. I stomped back into my office. "Can't go. I'm busy."

"Actually, you're not. But okay."

I threw myself into my chair, vowing not to look at the invitation. I lasted five minutes. "Maggie!"

"Yeah, boss, I have your tux right here."

Great. This was my chance to rectify a few things with Lily Gracen.

Once and for all.

Lily

The terrace of the Griffith Observatory was great for many things, including its stunning views of nighttime LA. But decked out in spotlights and caviar towers and champagne fountains, it was magnificent. That was before the celebrities and Fortune 500 CEOs who'd flown in from around the globe added their dazzle to the occasion.

After two weeks of hard publicity, tonight was the official launch party stroke fund-raiser for SDM's compression algorithm. And my final appearance as the ambassador for the most talked about development in the tech world. After tonight I was free. I'd never need to set eyes on Chance Donovan, or my stepfather again.

Even though the latter thought brought a pang of pain, I was okay with it. For the first time in my life, I could truly move forward with no baggage.

I closed on the sale of the abandoned drive-in movie theater today, and immediately applied for permission to convert it into offices. I was starting my own tech company and even though I was scared spitless, I was also excited.

If nothing else, starting a company from the ground up would take my mind off thinking about Caleb.

Whoever said time healed all wounds was a dotard. With every passing day, the hole in my chest grew wider, deeper. There were times when I feared the thing could just expire from the brutal trauma it endured daily, simply because it craved one night of perfection that would never be repeated.

But did you make absolutely sure it couldn't be repeated? Or did you shut the door because you were hurt and never looked back?

Those lingering questions were the reason I hadn't erased his last message from two weeks ago from my phone. Or maybe I was just a glutton for punishment.

Had he moved on? Was he currently buried neck deep in a new exciting case?

"I have no idea what it does, but I hear it's revolutionary. What did they call it again?"

"They called it the Angel Algorithm," a deep, magnificent voice said.

Dear God. His voice...

"Why *Angel*?"

"Because it's the creator's middle name," Caleb replied.

"Oh, how special," the female guest gushed.

"I couldn't agree more. She's one of a kind."

Heart in my throat, I turned around. He stood six feet away. Resplendent in a black tux and snowy white shirt. His face looked a little thinner but the designer stubble and slightly windswept hair worked for him so splendidly, I couldn't have pried my eyes off him if an earthquake cratered the ground beneath my feet.

The crowd seemed to part between us, and he loomed, magnificent, over me. "That was right, wasn't it?"

Breath totally depleted, I nodded. "Short for Angela. Chance let me name it." After witnessing the code that would make him and his company billions, he'd been so ecstatic he'd allowed me to name it. Regardless of how our relationship had begun, it was ending on my terms, with an achievement I was proud of. I'd chosen to let go of all grudges.

"It's a beautiful name." Caleb's voice was a little gruff, his eyes a fierce blue that blazed over me from my crown to my feet and back again. "Hello, Lily."

"Hi," I whispered.

"You look…incredible."

"Thank you." In honor of tonight, I'd gone a different way with my clothes. Dressed top to toe in white, the only splash of color were the red soles of my white platform heels. Diamond-and-pearl pins secured my slicked back hair, and even the choker around my neck was white leather.

Caleb's eyes lingered there the longest, setting my body aflame. "Lily, can we talk?"

Say no. Save yourself more heartache. "Yes."

Relief drenched his face. He started to reach for me. Someone bumped into me, sending me one stumble forward.

"Okay, enough of this shit," Caleb growled. He relieved me of my half-finished champagne glass, meshed his fingers with mine and tugged me through the crowd.

"Where are you taking me?"

"You'll see."

"But…I can't leave the party."

"You've given Donovan the algorithm. You've done his speeches. You don't owe him a thing. Besides, we need to revisit our last conversation in Lake Tahoe. There are a few things I never got around to saying." He gripped me tighter as I navigated the steps to the lower level, then increased his pace again.

"God, I haven't missed this bossy side of you at all."

I tried to project irritation but the wild hum in my veins wasn't anger. It was...*joy.*

"Sure you have. Or you wouldn't be hurrying to keep up with me."

He was right. I would go anywhere with this man, but at what price?

"I still want to know where we're going."

"We're here," he replied in a hushed voice, then pushed the door open.

I entered, and gasped. "We can't be in here," I whispered halfheartedly. But my excitement tripled as I gazed up at the stunning constellation splashed across the planetarium roof.

His fingers trailed up my wrists, my arms, to cup my shoulders. I redirected my gaze to his, saw the raw emotion stamped on his face.

"I'm fucking pissed at you."

I gasped. "What?"

"You heard me. But God, I've also missed you. So much," he confessed raggedly.

I stopped myself from blurting out that I'd missed him, too. "Have you? You were shitty to me."

His face clouded with pain. "Believe me, I know. I'd do anything to take it all back."

My throat clogged. Excitement faded and harrowing pain rushed at me. "Would you? Why?"

"Because you didn't deserve it. Not a single one of the things I threw at you."

"Are you sure? Because there's no shame in admitting you don't have room in your life...for me." It hurt me to say it, but it needed to be said.

He shook his head vehemently. "That's not—"

"I saw how devastated you were when you told

me about your mom. You blame yourself for her. You moved heaven and earth for her and she still died, and after that you were never going to become so wrapped up in anyone else. Am I right?"

He stared down at me for the longest time. Then he exhaled harshly. "Yes. I'd love to say I fought hard to shut people out, but…after she died, it was easy to close the door, to bottle the pain and become the lone wolf no one depended on. Until Kirsten."

My heart twisted with pain for him. For me. "And she let you down, too."

His mouth tightened. "I don't want to talk about her. She's not important. Not anymore. She was just another crutch I used to distance myself. The option to walk away on my own terms before things got heavy with anyone was mine alone. I was okay with it. Until I met you. You forced me to take a long, hard look at myself."

My lungs flattened. "Caleb…"

"Walking away from you was the hardest thing I've ever done, Lily," he confessed forcefully.

Remembering brought more pain. "Then why did you?"

"I let my guard down with you. My instincts warned me about Miranda but I saw how close you were to your team. To her. I knew you would be hurt if it was her and I didn't want you to experience that pain. I hesitated when I could've acted sooner. Then the breach happened and all I could think about was that I could've lost you. In the end I did anyway by pushing you away, when I should've pulled you close."

"I thought you were into her. Miranda."

Caleb's fingers brushed my throat and I realized I was clinging to his wrists. "I'm into one particular pint-size blonde, with a heart of gold, the courage of a lion and a body designed to stop traffic."

"She's into you, too, but she was terrified all you'd ever want was to be a fixer. That she wouldn't be able to compete with your calling. You chose to do what you do to help people but also to stay connected to your mother. I… I didn't know if I could compete with that."

"The moment you walked into my life, the competition was over. I would've come after you whether you were a client or not. My heart and my soul craved you even before I knew what was happening. That second time in Lake Tahoe was my piss-poor way of telling you I couldn't live without you."

"Oh, Caleb."

"I've been wretched without you. The thought of waking up every morning for the rest of my life without you…" He stopped and shook his head, urgent hands cupping my cheeks to tilt my gaze to his. "If there's any part of you that feels a fraction of that, please give me a chance to make us both happy."

Bright, shining hope billowed through me. "Do you mean that?"

"With every bone in my body," he breathed.

"Oh, my God."

Fevered eyes pierced me. "Is that… Are you considering it, Lily?"

"I don't need to. I was thinking of what it would be like to wake up each day with you."

His fingers trembled against my cheek. "And?"

"I would love that, Caleb. So very much."

A blinding smile erupted. "God, Lily… I love you."

Hope turned to joy, filling my battered spaces with

new, vibrant life, and my eyes with tears. "I love you, too," I wailed.

Caleb stared at me for a stupefied moment; then my big, magnificent man snatched me in his arms, but not before I caught a suspicious sheen in his eyes.

He fused his lips to mine, and my heart sighed with happiness. Still bound in his arms, I felt him moving. Felt him sink into a seat before he placed me before him.

His hands worshipped my face, my neck, my fingers. Adoring eyes pinned me as he slid his hands under my dress.

"I saw you on TV." His fingers drifted up my thighs.

"Yes, I've been doing a lot of that lately," I whispered.

He nodded. "You looked…incredible."

"Yes, you said that already," I teased.

He hummed as he skimmed the edge of my panties. "I had this fantasy as I watched you give that *Tech-Crunch* interview."

"Yeah?" I was beginning to pant and I didn't even care.

He hooked two fingers into the lace and dragged it down my legs. "Hmm. You were rattling off all these big tech words and numbers. And I promised myself if I ever got you back, I would have you recite the Fibonnaci Sequence while I fucked you long and slow."

My gasp echoed around the large room. "Oh, my God."

He tapped my legs. I stepped out of my panties, and he stuffed them into his jacket pocket. "That's not all. You would be wearing nothing but a choker, those boxy glasses and black heels you wore for the *Wired* cover shoot when you announced you were starting your own company. I'm incredibly proud of you for that, by the way."

My heart threatened to burst with happiness. "Did you watch *all* my interviews?"

"Every single one. Twice. I bought all the magazines, too. I've had a very busy afternoon." He plucked a condom from his wallet, handed it to me, then reached beneath his cummerbund and lowered his zipper.

"Wow. If I didn't know better, I'd say you were obsessed with me, Mr. Steele."

His eyes clung to mine. "It's more than an obsession. You're my reason for breathing."

My fingers shook as I tore open the condom. Then the shaking suffused my whole body as he took out his big, beautiful cock.

I leaned over him, kissed his gorgeous lips before bending lower to kiss the crown of his penis. His strangled curse was music to my ears.

The moment I glided the condom on, he pulled me close, tugged my legs on either side of his lap, and he stared up at me with eyes shining with unfettered love. I braced my hands on his shoulders and sank down, slowly, excruciatingly impaling myself on him. His groan mingled with mine.

When he was fully seated inside me, he held me still.

"There are over a billion stars above our heads right now. But I bet we could touch every one of them if we tried really, really hard."

I cupped his jaw in my hands. "I'd love nothing better than to reach for the stars with you. Oh, Caleb. I love you."

"I love you, too. I'm going to spend the rest of my life making you incredibly, sublimely happy," he vowed.

I sealed my lips to his and silently promised that, for as long as the sun rose each morning, I would love and worship him, too.

* * * * *

COMING SOON!

We really hope you enjoyed reading this book. If you're looking for more romance, be sure to head to the shops when new books are available on

Thursday
23rd August

To see which titles are coming soon, please visit
millsandboon.co.uk

LET'S TALK
Romance

For exclusive extracts, competitions
and special offers, find us online:

f facebook.com/millsandboon

⊙ @millsandboonuk

🐦 @millsandboon

Or get in touch on 0844 844 1351*

For all the latest titles coming soon, visit
millsandboon.co.uk/nextmonth